All AudioCraft books are proudly printed, bound, and manufactured in the United States of America, utilizing American resources.

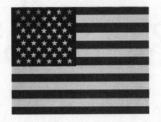

USA

NORTH CAROLINA
NIGHT CREATURES

"I have to tell you that you're my favorite author! I never liked reading before, until I read IDAHO ICE BEAST. I loved that book, and I even did a book report on it!"

-Mark R., age 10, Oregon

"Your dogs are so cute. Your books are good, but I like your dogs, too. You should write a book about them."

-Jasmine J., age 13, South Carolina

"I know you get a ton of mail, but I hope you read this. Everyone in my school is in love with your books! Our library has a bunch of them, but they're never on the shelves when I go to get another one."

-Preston N., age 9, Michigan

"We had a book fair at our school, and they had a bunch of your books. I bought three of them and I read all of them! They're great! I'm going to buy more when we have another book fair."

-Rachel S., age 11, Pennsylvania

"We took a vacation and went to Chillermania and you were there! Do you remember me? My name is Bryson, and I had blue shirt. I bought six books and a hat! My dad says we will come again next summer."

-Sam W., age 12, Tennessee

"Keep writing! I love all of your books, especially the Michigan Chillers, because that's where I'm from!"
-Aaron P., age 10, Michigan

"Thank you for writing me back! My friends didn't believe you would, but I showed them your letter and the bookmark you sent. That was so cool!"

-Kate B., age 10, Indiana

"My favorite book is SAVAGE DINOSAURS OF SOUTH DAKOTA. I think you should make movies out of all your books, especially this one!"

-Keith A., Age 11, New Jersey

"I started reading the Freddie Fernortner books, and now I'm reading all of your American Chillers books! I love all of them! I can't decide which one is my favorite."

-Jenna T., age 9, Minnesota

"After I read VIRTUAL VAMPIRES OF VERMONT, I had strange dreams. Does that happen to anyone else, or is it just me?"

-Anders B., age 12, Texas

"I read your books every night just before I go to bed. I have six of my own, but I borrow more from the library. I love all of them! Keep writing!"

-Annette O., age 11, Nebraska

Got something cool to say about Johnathan Rand's books? Let us know, and we might publish it right here! Send your short blurb to:

Chiller Blurbs
281 Cool Blurbs Ave.
Topinabee, MI 49791

Other books by Johnathan Rand:

#41: North Carolina Night Creatures

Johnathan Rand

An AudioCraft Publishing, Inc. book

Book storage and warehouses provided by Chillermania!©
Indian River, Michigan

American Chillers #41: North Carolina Night Creatures
ISBN 13-digit: 978-1-893699-17-5

Librarians/Media Specialists:
PCIP/MARC records available **free of charge** at
www.americanchillers.com

Cover illustration by Dwayne Harris
Cover layout and design by Sue Harring

Printed in USA

NORTH CAROLINA
NIGHT CREATURES

VISIT CHILLERMANIA!

WORLD HEADQUARTERS FOR BOOKS BY JOHNATHAN RAND!

Yooperland

Indian River

Alpena

Traverse City

MICHIGAN

CHILLERMANIA!

**I-75 Exit 313
then south
1 mile!**

Mt. Pleasant

Bay City

Grand Rapids

Lansing

Kalamazoo

Detroit

Visit the HOME for books by Johnathan Rand! Featuring books, hats, shirts, bookmarks and other cool stuff not available anywhere else in the world! Plus, watch the American Chillers website for news of special events and signings at *CHILLERMANIA!* with author Johnathan Rand! Located in northern lower Michigan, on I-75! Take exit 313 . . . then south 1 mile! For more info, call (231) 238-0338. And be afraid! Be veeeery afraaaaaaiiiid . . . .

Whenever you wake up screaming in the middle of the night, you're bound to create a stir in your household. But when you wake up screaming and fall off the bed? Well, that's even worse.

And that's what happened to me one night in May. Or morning, I should say, to make myself perfectly clear, because the clock on my night stand read 3:42 AM. So, to be completely truthful, I wasn't awakened in the middle of the night. It was very early in the morning.

But that really doesn't make any difference.

All I remember was being chased by horrible creatures. In my nightmare, I was trying to run from them, trying to get away, but I couldn't move my legs fast enough. It was like I was trying to run in mud. The creatures were big: the size of humans, and they had claws like animals and wings like bats. They swarmed all around me, screeching and wailing. In my dream, I was screaming . . . but I didn't know that it was a dream. To me, it was very, very real.

And terrifying.

But a sharp pain to my head knocked the wicked fantasy out of my mind, and I found myself in the darkness, the shred of a shrill scream on my tongue. My head was throbbing. I was sweating, and I was confused.

Where did they go? I wondered in a panic, snapping my head around, ready to dive for cover.

A distant patter of thumps quickly became a thunder of footsteps. A door burst open, and light flared. My eyes burned, and I winced, shadowing my face with my forearm.

I was in my bedroom, of course, but I was on the floor. Dad and Mom stood in my bedroom doorway, looking worried and concerned. My

12

oldest sister, Shaina, stood behind Mom, peering around her. Next to Shaina was Abby, who is one year older than me. Dad was in his blue pajamas; Shaina, Abby, and Mom were in their nightgowns. For a brief instant, they all looked like pale ghosts.

"Hunter!" Mom exclaimed. "Are you all right?!?!"

I moved my arm and rubbed the sore spot on my head. I'd fallen out of bed and most likely banged my head on the hardwood floor.

"I . . . I was having a nightmare," I stammered. "There were all sorts of weird creatures chasing after me, and I couldn't get away. I guess I fell out of bed."

"Smooth move, knucklehead," Shaina sneered, rolling her sleepy eyes.

"Hush, Shaina," Mom said, glancing at my sister. Then, she stepped toward me and knelt down. She felt my head with the palm of her hand.

"Ouch," I said.

"You're going to have an egg there," Mom said, "but I think you'll be fine. Just a bump."

"You're lucky nothing fell out," Abby said.

"That's enough, girls," Dad grumbled. "Go back to bed."

My sisters vanished in the dark hall, stumbling sleepily to their bedrooms.

"Well, now that we know the world's not ending," Dad said, "I'm going back to bed." He turned and walked away.

"Are you sure you're all right?" Mom asked me.

"Yeah," I said, and I climbed to my feet.

"I'll get you a glass of water," she said. "You get back in bed."

Mom left, and I crawled back into bed. The sheets and covers were a mess from my kicking and thrashing. I rearranged the covers and pulled them to my neck. Then, Mom returned, holding a glass of water. She sat on the bed and handed me the glass. I sipped. It was cool and refreshing and felt good on my dry throat.

"Thanks," I said, between gulps.

"What was your dream about?" Mom asked.

"Monsters," I replied, after I took another gulp of water. "They were chasing me, and I couldn't get away."

"That's because of all those scary books you read," Mom said with a faint smile.

I shook my head. "No, it's not," I replied.

14

But then again, I couldn't be sure. I love to read scary books, and maybe they were the reason I had so many nightmares. Some of the books I read were so terrifying that I had to sleep with the light on. Still, I love reading them, and I wasn't going to quit, even if they did give me scary dreams.

I drank half the glass of water and then placed it on my night stand.

"Well," Mom said as she stood. "Try to get back to sleep. And try not to have any more bad dreams."

"Okay," I said.

Mom shut off the light and closed the door, leaving it open just a crack. A thin sliver of amber glowed between the door and the molding, coming from the nightlight in the hall. The light was welcome and comforting, and the darkness in my room didn't seem so scary. I closed my eyes . . . but only for a moment.

Suddenly, I heard a faint scratching on my window screen, and my eyes flew open. The window was closed, of course, because the night was chilly. But I could still hear the faint scratching against the screen on the other side of the glass pane, like the sound of a metal zipper slowing being pulled up and then down.

Up . . . and down . . . .

And why did I decide to get up to see what it was?

I don't know, especially after having such a horrifying nightmare. But I knew that if I called for Mom and Dad, they'd probably get mad when they discovered it was only some insect or moth on the screen. No doubt Shaina and Abby would come running, too, and they would make fun of me for days, telling everyone that I got scared by a puny little bug.

Up . . . and down . . . .

So, very slowly, I climbed out of bed.

I crept to the window.

Up . . . and down . . . .

Slowly, using the index finger of my right hand, I pulled open the drape . . . and stared in disbelief at the creature on the wire screen.

2

When I saw what was on the screen, I flinched. Then, I drew in a quick breath and held it, surprised and shocked at what I was seeing.

"Wow," I whispered.

It was only a beetle . . . but he was huge. He was as big as my thumb and probably the biggest insect I'd ever seen in my life. Ever since I was a little kid, I had been fascinated with bugs. I was always catching them and putting them in jars and trying to find out their proper names. In some cases, I memorized their Latin names, speaking them out loud to myself for practice, so I would be sure to say them right. At school, it was fun to tell my friends that I had caught a Nematocera Culicidae. Most of my friends would frown and wonder what in the world I was talking about when I used words like this. Of course, a Nematocera Culicidae is simply the Latin name for an ordinary mosquito, but my friends didn't know that.

But the beetle crawling around on my screen? I had no idea what it was. All I knew was that he was gigantic, and if it hadn't been the middle of the night, I would have rushed outside with my insect net and a jar to catch him and keep him, at least for a day or two. I would have loved to get a better look at him in the daylight.

However, it was dark. Even in the faint glow of the streetlights, I couldn't see the insect's features, except the silhouette of his fat, oblong body and his six legs, along with two, fat antennae protruding from his head.

I watched him crawl on the screen for an inch or two, stop, then crawl some more, then stop again. I heard the soothing, pulsating sound of nearby crickets in the bushes beneath my window.

I reached up with my hand, extending my

index finger. Just as I was about to touch the window, the bug flew off with a furious clapping sound. His wings were loud, and the creature sounded like a tiny airplane taking flight. He was so big that I could see his shape in the glow beneath the street light, and I watched as the insect landed in the yard.

Too bad it's not daytime, I thought. If it was, I'd go out and catch that thing in a jar.

I climbed back into bed and closed my eyes. Soon, I fell asleep.

In the morning, I'd forgotten all about the dream I'd had the night before. I forgot about the insect on the screen. The only thing I was aware of when I awoke was being hungry. So, I tumbled out of bed, found my slippers, and made my way to the kitchen.

The house was quiet, and I was the only one awake. Shaina and Abby always slept in. Usually, Mom or Dad had to wake them up to get them out of bed.

But not me. During the summer, I was always up early, usually right when the sun came up. Summer meant no school, and I was going to make the most of every day.

I poured a bowl of cereal and grabbed a gallon of milk from the fridge. Then, I sat at the kitchen table to eat and read the back of the cereal box. Cereal boxes always have something interesting to say, even if it's only the nutritional guidelines. And once in a while, there is a prize hidden inside the box. Mostly, it's just useless junk. But it's still fun to get something free.

Something I read on the box triggered my memory, and I suddenly remembered the insect I'd discovered on the screen the night before. Once again, I wished that I'd discovered the creature during the daylight hours. I would have caught him, for sure. It was too bad he was gone for good.

I also remembered falling out of bed, and I reached up to find a lump on the back of my head. It was a little sore, but not bad.

After finishing my cereal, I rinsed the bowl and spoon and put them in the dishwasher. Then, I returned the milk to the fridge. I pushed away the memory of the beetle from the night before, and another thought entered my mind.

What am I going to do today? I wondered. It had been sunny and hot for the past few days, but I'd heard that rain was supposed to move in today.

Most likely, that would mean I'd be inside and not playing outdoors with my friends. If it rained only a little, that wouldn't be any big deal. But Mom and Dad didn't like me playing outside during thunderstorms. They were always afraid I'd get hit by lightning.

I strode through the kitchen, into the living room, and to the big window that faces our front yard. It was getting light out. Mom's blue van was parked in the driveway, and there were two cars parked in the driveway across the street. The sky was covered by a layer of flat, gray clouds. Although it wasn't raining yet, it looked like the weather forecasters were going to be right, after all.

I was about to head to my bedroom and change into my clothes when something in the gloomy yard caught my attention.

A pile of dirt.

In the middle of the front yard, there was a small pile of dirt as if the lawn had been chewed up, or someone had dug a hole. I moved closer to the window and peered curiously at the strange sight, trying to remember what had happened the day before that might have caused the earth in the front yard to be disturbed. Mom or Dad wouldn't have done anything like that, I was sure. Dad freaks out if you mess with his lawn. He keeps it mowed and watered, so it always looks perfect. If my sisters or I would have dug a hole or somehow damaged the lawn, Dad would have grounded us until we graduated high school. Which, for me, was a long time, because I'm only eleven.

At the time, I'd completely forgotten about the giant beetle that I'd found buzzing at my screen the night before. I'd forgotten that the insect had flown off and landed somewhere in the yard.

Those were things that I would remember later, when I started to figure things out, when I began to put two and two together. That was when an ordinary, average day in Raleigh, North Carolina would take some very strange—and horrifying—turns.

3

Still puzzled about the mound of dirt in the yard, I pulled myself away from the window and padded back to my bedroom. I flipped on the light and changed into a pair of jeans and a T-shirt, found my tennis shoes, and slipped them on.

I turned off the light. Just as I entered the hall, a scratching sound behind me caught my attention. I stopped and turned, gazing around my murky room.

I clicked the bedroom light on again.

Scratch. Scra-Scratch.

It was coming from my window. Something

was scratching at the screen.

I walked to it, reached out, and drew the curtain back with my hand, expecting to see the beetle or some other sort of insect.

There was nothing there.

I held the drape open and gazed into the yard, dimly lit by the coming of the day. Once again, my eyes caught the small mound of dirt in the middle of the lawn.

After standing at my window for a few moments and not hearing the sound again, I let go of the curtain and allowed it to close. Then, I turned and walked out of my bedroom, clicking off the light as I left.

I walked by Shaina's bedroom. Even though her door was closed, I could hear her snoring. She snores just about every night, and she sounds like a semi-truck. She snores louder than my dad.

In the living room closet, I found my gray sweatshirt and pulled it over my head. Quietly, I slipped out the front door.

The morning air was cool, but it wouldn't be long before summer's heat awoke from its slumber. Summer days can be unbearably hot in North Carolina, even on cloudy days like this one.

I leapt off the porch and jogged across the lawn, stopping as I reached the pile of dirt. I kneeled in the cool, damp grass.

The dirt was clumped in a small, beach ball-sized area. And it appeared freshly-moved, too. I grabbed a clump of it and let the grains of gritty sand fall through my fingers. Then, I turned and looked at my bedroom window.

Somewhere, a bird called. I could also hear the sound of cars on the distant freeway, a familiar, droning hum that I heard often. For some reason, it sounded strange.

I looked around the neighborhood.

There was no one else in sight, no one moving. Even grouchy, old Mr. Millard, our next door neighbor, hadn't been out to get his newspaper. It was still rolled up on the first step of his porch.

I looked at my window again. Beneath it, and growing all along the front of the house to the porch, was a band of thick, leafy, spinach-colored shrubbery.

Something had been scratching on my window. Last night, it had been a beetle.

But he'd flown away, I thought. He'd flown

away and landed—

I looked at the small pile of disturbed earth by my feet.

—here. He landed in the grass, right here.

This morning, just moments ago when I was inside, something else had been scratching at the screen.

I walked toward my bedroom window and stopped at the edge of the shrubbery. I peered at the screen and all around the window pane, looking for signs of the insect. I thought that perhaps he'd returned, and maybe he'd made the same scratching sounds just moments before, when I'd been in my room.

No beetle.

I was disappointed, because I thought I might have another chance to grab him. He would have been easy to catch, and I was certain he wasn't dangerous. I didn't think he'd bite me or anything. Plus, both of my sisters hated bugs and spiders. It would have been fun to freak them out!

I turned and stared back at the mound of disturbed earth, the clump of dirt on the cool, dew-covered grass.

Was it possible that the beetle somehow did

that? I wondered. He was big, for sure . . . but it didn't seem possible that it would have been able to create such a large disturbance in the lawn.

Suddenly, I felt a sharp, painful, stinging sensation on my ankle, just above my tennis shoe . . . and that's the moment that I realized that maybe the beetle was dangerous, after all . . . .

I yelped and jumped back from the bushes, reaching down to swat the giant beetle—or whatever it was—off my leg.

There was nothing there.

I looked all over my shoe, my sock, my pant leg . . . but I didn't find an insect.

Moving closer to the bushes, I searched the leafy vegetation. I didn't find an insect, but suddenly, near my feet, a small branch moved.

I took a step back and knelt down. As I did, the shrubbery exploded, and an enormous, human-sized insect attacked!

Except it wasn't an insect at all. It was Lindsay Morford, one of my best friends! She had been hiding in the bushes all along, waiting for me!

When she leapt out, she roared like a lion and raised her arms like a bear. Yeah, she surprised me, but I can't say that I was scared. She looked funny, and there were curled, green leaves and jagged twigs on her baseball cap and stuck to her gray sweatshirt.

"Hahahaha!" she said, lowering her hands and placing them on her hips. "Now, that was funny!"

I smiled and nodded. "You surprised me, all right," I said. "I thought you were a giant beetle."

Lindsay looked down at herself and then looked at me and rolled her eyes. "I think I can see the resemblance," she said, brushing herself off and adjusting her ball cap. "But I don't feel like a bug."

"How long were you hiding there?" I asked, pointing to the bushes.

Lindsay shrugged. "Oh, ten minutes, I guess. I got up early to go fishing with one of my older brothers, but he got called in to work, so we didn't go. I figured you'd still be in bed, so I came over here to freak you out. I tried scraping on the screen with my fingernails to scare you awake, but it didn't work."

I shook my head. "I heard you," I replied. "But I was already up. I thought that the sound might be coming from a huge beetle that was on my screen last night."

Lindsay's eyes lit up. "I saw a huge beetle last night, too!" she said. "In fact, I caught it, and I put it in a shoe box!"

My jaw fell.

"You did?" I asked. "Where is it?"

"In our garage," Lindsay replied, hiking her thumb over her shoulder. "I left him there last night. I guess I forgot about him until just now. Wanna see him?"

"Are you kidding?!?!" I asked. "I wanted so bad to catch him last night, but he flew away. Besides, I don't think my parents would have been real happy about me running around outside in my pajamas, chasing a bug around in the middle of the night."

"Come on," Lindsay said. "I'll show you the one I caught."

We walked, side by side, to Lindsay's house, completely unaware of the awful surprise we were about to find waiting for us in a dark corner of Lindsay's garage.

"Where did you catch the beetle?" I asked Lindsay.

We were walking along the sidewalk. It was still early, but the neighborhood was slowly waking. The birds, of course, were always first, chittering and talking and making a ruckus. But as the sun rises, other things come alive. The sounds of the freeway in the distance get a little louder as more and more vehicles pile onto the roadways, clogging the arteries of Raleigh. Front doors whisk open and slam closed in the neighborhood, and sleepy people stumble to their cars and mailboxes. Some people, like old Mrs. Carpenter at the end of the block, walk their dog every single morning.

"I found the beetle in our driveway," Lindsay replied. "He was just crawling along. I couldn't believe how big he was. I caught him in an old shoe box, and I figured I would show him to you this morning. I thought we might try to find out what kind he is."

"I think it's a giganticus flybugguss," I said with a grin.

"A what?" replied Lindsay.

"I was just trying to be funny," I said. "I was trying to come up with a Latin-sounding name."

"Whatever," Lindsay said, smiling and rolling her eyes.

Lindsay's home is only three blocks from mine, so it didn't take us long to get there. She lives in a white, two-story house. It has an attached, single-car garage, but the big roll-up door was closed when we arrived. We entered through a smaller door on the side. The garage has no other doors and no windows, and it was dark and musty inside. The air was cool and smelled stale and damp, with a hint of oil and grease.

"Mom wouldn't let me bring the beetle into the house," Lindsay explained as she pushed open the door. "She was worried that he'd get out, and we'd never find him. Then, he'd be crawling all around the house."

The open door allowed morning's gray light to wash through the shadowy garage. Lindsay's mom has a blue van almost identical to my mom's, and the vehicle was taking up a large portion of the space.

Lindsay pointed. "I put the box up there, in front of Mom's van," she said, squeezing her way between the van and a metal shelf cluttered with old tools and paint cans. "He's in a shoe box on the floor."

"Don't you have a light in here?" I asked, following closely behind Lindsay, feeling my way along with my hands.

"We do," Lindsay replied, "but the bulb burned out a few days ago. I'd replace it, but I can't reach it. Mom says she will, but she hasn't gotten around to it yet."

We reached the front of the van, and there wasn't much space between the hood of the vehicle and the back wall of the garage. Because it was so dark, I couldn't see anything but the silhouette of the van and some garden tools hanging on the wall. The smell of engine oil and grease tickled my nostrils.

"Let me see," Lindsay said curiously, speaking to herself. "It's around here somewhere."

"It's so dark," I said, "I don't know how you can see anything."

"Yeah," Lindsay agreed, "but it'll only take a moment for our eyes to adjust. Besides, it's a shoe box. It's right around here, somewhere. Oh! Here it is."

I saw Lindsay's dark form kneel down and then stand up. She was, of course, now holding the box. But in the gloomy confines of the garage, I could make out only a fuzzy shape.

"Wait a minute," she said, backing up and bumping into me. I took a few steps backward toward the door and into the light. Lindsay followed, carrying the shoe box.

"Look at this!" Lindsay said. "The thing ate through the box! He's gone!"

She held the box out for me to see. Not only had the insect chewed a hole through the cardboard, but much of the box had been mangled.

"Holy cow," I said quietly. "He chewed right through the cardboard. I guess he really wanted out."

"Rats," Lindsay said, glancing around the garage. "Now, he's gone, and we'll never find him."

And that's when something moved on the shelf to my left. I turned, but it was already too late. A giant insect—the size of a house cat—leapt into the air and landed on my chest, sinking his razor-sharp pincers into my shoulder!

I jumped back, but slammed into the van. Hard. There was nowhere I could go. Throwing my arms up in a frenzy, I swatted frantically at the insect on my upper chest. Then, the creature sprang again, this time using my shoulder as a launching pad. In the next instant, the giant insect had vanished.

I turned and spun to see Lindsay, grinning from ear to ear.

"Man, you sure get freaked out easily," she said, just as calm and cool as ever.

My heart was thrashing, and I was still leaning against the van. My palms were pressed against the chilly metal. My breaths came in quick hammer-gasps.

"What . . . what was that?" I stammered.

"That was Shadow," Lindsay said, very matter-of-factly, as if I should have known exactly what she was talking about.

"Shadow?"

"Yeah," Lindsay said. "He's a stray cat that's been living around here for the last few weeks. Mom wants to take him to the animal shelter, but Dad says Shadow is doing a good job catching mice in the garage. He puts food out for him, and Shadow sticks around. I named him 'Shadow' because he's all black, and he stays out of sight most of the time. We hardly ever see him. 'Shadow' seemed like a fitting name for him."

"Man," I said, leaning forward, away from the van. "He sure surprised me. I thought I was being attacked by a giant insect."

"Speaking of giant insects," Lindsay said, holding up the box. "It looks like I won't get to show you the one I caught after all."

I leaned closer. The box hadn't simply been chewed—it had been mangled. One entire end had been torn to shreds, as if it had been attacked by a whirling razor blade.

"That's really weird," I said. Lindsay handed the shredded box to me, and I rolled it over in my hands. "You'd think that if a bug wanted out, he'd just chew a hole big enough to escape. Whatever was in this box didn't just chew a hole. He shredded it to pieces."

"I wonder where he went," said Lindsay. She turned her head downward and gazed at the floor. Her eyes leapt back and forth.

"He's long gone by now," I said. "Or maybe the cat ate him."

"Ewww!" Lindsay said. "I hadn't thought about that."

"I bet he was crunchy," I said.

"Gross! Stop it!"

"I bet he sounded like a potato chip being eaten," I continued. "Crunch-crunch-crunch."

Lindsay put her hands over her ears. "Lalalalala," she sang. "I can't hear a word you're saying! Lalalalala!"

I smiled. "Okay," I said. "Enough about crunchy bugs."

Lindsay uncovered her ears and lowered her hands. "Now," she said, looking around. "Where did Shadow go? He sure scared the heck out of you."

"I think I must've scared him just as bad," I said with a grin.

We both had a good laugh about it. I had to admit that it was pretty funny, to be scared so badly by a stray cat.

But soon, we wouldn't be laughing.

Soon, we wouldn't be joking.

We would be screaming.

We searched the dark garage for a few minutes.

"Shadow?" Lindsay called out as she dropped to her hands and knees. She peered beneath the van.

Seconds ticked past.

"Anything?" I asked

"Nope," she replied, getting to her feet. "But it's no big deal. He's around here, somewhere. He's kind of a loner that way, and he likes to keep to himself a lot. He'll show up when he wants to."

"Or when you leave food out for him," I said.

"Hey," Lindsay said, her eyes brightening. "That's a good idea. I'll be right back."

Lindsay left me standing inside the garage while she went into her house. I leaned against the blue van, listening, watching, waiting. There was nothing to hear except the usual birds outside and the faint, electric-like hum of the distant freeway.

Lindsay had placed the mangled cardboard shoe box on the shelf, and I picked it up. Not only had it been torn to shreds, but there were deep, angry scratch marks all over the inside.

I peered closer, inspecting the tattered cardboard, noticing that the tears were clean and smooth.

Whatever did this, I thought, it sure has some sharp claws. Or teeth. I sure wouldn't want the thing clawing or gnawing at me.

Without warning, a dark form appeared on the hood of the van. It made no sound, and, I must admit, caused me to nearly jump out of my skin.

I let out a sigh of relief and smiled.

"You," I said to the cat sitting on the hood, stoic and straight like a little onyx statue, sculptured and honed to perfection like a piece of black granite that would stand to weather the elements for millions of years.

In reality, though, it was just Shadow the stray cat, furry and warm, made out of flesh. Living in the garage and outdoors, he was probably dirty and probably had fleas.

"You scared me," I said, grinning at the cat. "That's twice. I owe you."

The cat remained motionless except for his tail, which twisted slowly like a cobra's head, back and forth, back and forth in a hypnotic motion. His metallic golden eyes with dark, teardrop pupils glared at me.

I returned the mangled box to the shelf and took a step toward Shadow, toward the front of the van. I half expected the animal to run off again. After all, he was a stray cat. Strays tend to avoid people. Some of them, particularly the feral ones that live in the woods, don't like humans at all. I felt bad for them, not having homes or human friends, no place warm to go in the winter or stay dry in a thunderstorm.

But Shadow didn't seem to be like that. When I raised my arm and reached out to pet him, he leaned into my hand, closed his eyes, and pressed his ears against my fingers.

"You like that, kitty-cat?" I said as I stroked the back of his ears with my fingers.

As if he could understand me, Shadow began to purr. Then, he stood and arched his back, and I moved my arm down to his neck and, using my fingernails, scratched gently at his bony, rigid spine. Shadow responded by purring louder and arching his back even more. He looked like a black, furry horseshoe.

"You seem pretty friendly," I said. "You don't seem like a stray at all."

Suddenly, Shadow froze, as if something had caught his attention. Then, in a single, graceful leap, he bounded from the hood of the van and landed on the metal shelf against the wall. His movements were as quiet as smoke, as smooth as glass. He turned and stared . . . but not at me.

He was looking at the cement floor below. His tail swished slowly back and forth.

Then, it stopped.

Shadow remained frozen, motionless, a black stone statue captured by time, a living photograph.

A scratching sound came from beneath the van, and a chill iced my skin like arctic electricity.

Scrrrrrrr—

It sounded like metal on stone, a sharp instrument against a solid, heavy substance: like metal against rock.

Or claws against cement, I thought.

Shadow sat next to the mangled box, and my mind skipped over dozens of images in an instant. Mostly, they were the images of the beetle at my window, the beetle flying off into the night in a plastic clapping of wings. Of razor-sharp claws tearing into Lindsay's cardboard box and the mysterious mound of dirt that had appeared overnight in our yard.

And then, to my horror, something appeared on the cement, just inches from my feet . . . .

Right away, I knew I wasn't looking at the insect I'd spotted the night before. Oh, the thing at my feet was an insect, all right, but it was a lot bigger than the beetle I'd discovered on my screen. In fact, I would have to say that it was the same type of beetle, the very same kind . . . except the one I was now looking at was three or four times the size of the one that had been at my screen, the one that had flown off into the yard! It was all black, shiny and glossy, with long, thick legs. Each leg had claws, like curved, sharp knives. And the claws were wide and large, resembling that of a mole.

Clearly, this was an insect designed to fight and defend, to ravish and destroy, to seize its prey and never let go. I'd never seen a bug so big in my life.

But strangest of all were its wings. They were spread partially open, but they didn't look like normal insect wings. Rather, they were skin-like, long and wide, similar to the wings of a bat.

The beetle was crawling slowly, making dull scrit-scrit-scrit sounds with its fat claws. There's a kid at school that scrapes his fingernails along the blackboard just to annoy everyone. The sound makes me cringe every time he does it. That's what it sounded like as the beetle crawled along.

When the insect reached my tennis shoe, it stopped. It never occurred to me that I should lift my foot, just in case the thing wanted to bite me. But I think I was too surprised by what I was seeing. Half of me wanted to run away as fast as I could; the other half wanted to find something to capture the bug, so I could watch it for a while. Or show it off to some of my friends. Or scare Shaina and Abby! That would be the best! I'm sure they'd freak out if they saw a beetle that big!

The insect paused at my shoe, as if it had reached a brick wall. Then, it slowly scrambled over my foot and continued its way along the floor.

Meanwhile, Shadow sat on the shelf. He looked down, and his wiry tail waved back and forth.

Not far away, I heard a door close. Lindsay was coming back.

On the floor, the insect stopped moving.

On the shelf, Shadow's tail stopped moving. It remained taut and curved, bent like a furry, black question mark.

Shadow and I watched the beetle.

The beetle, it seemed, was watching Lindsay, although I couldn't see her yet. I could hear her footsteps coming closer, the careless slap of her tennis shoes on the pavement becoming louder and more pronounced.

"Lindsay, wait," I called out. "Stop."

The sounds of her footsteps ceased.

"What?" she replied.

"The beetle that you caught is right here, on the floor. He's almost out the door."

I heard a scuffing of feet.

"I can see him!" Lindsay said from outside. I still couldn't see her. "Can you catch him?"

"How?" I asked.

"Put the shoe box over him!" she replied.

"He's already chewed through it once," I said. "He'll chew through it again. He'll get out real easy."

"Don't move," Lindsay said. "I'll see if we have something else. Maybe a jar or a plastic container."

I heard shuffling feet as she hustled off. On the floor, near my shoe, the beetle remained motionless. On the shelf, Shadow looked down, his tail still frozen in that curious, question-mark shape, his penetrating eyes fixed on the insect.

Moments later, I heard a door swish open and then click shut.

"This one should be big enough," I heard Lindsay holler from the yard, although I still couldn't see her. Cautious footsteps, however, told me she was approaching.

On the floor of the garage, the giant beetle hadn't moved.

On the shelf, Shadow's tail began to sway back and forth in that curious, cobra-like fashion.

"I have a plastic container with a lid," Lindsay said. "I'll get him myself."

She wasn't going to have the time.

At that very moment, the beetle took flight. He didn't crouch and leap; he gave no warning at all. One minute he was on the cement floor near my foot, and the next minute he was airborne, a black blur of furious, clapping wings, the sound of playing cards in bicycle spokes. He vanished out the door in a black flash, and I could no longer see him.

But then came another sound:

Lindsay. She was screaming, screaming like I had never heard her scream before.

Shadow, frightened by Lindsay's screaming, leapt from the shelf, ricocheted off my shoulder, landed on the hood of the van, and bounded off into the darkness of the garage. Like the beetle, the cat had vanished.

Lindsay screamed one last time. Then, I heard a heavy thwak! The flapping of plastic wings continued, but the sound quickly drifted off as the insect flew away.

As if awaking from a daze, I sprang out the garage door.

"Lindsay?" I said, rushing toward her. "Are

you all right?"

She was on her knees in the grass, holding a green plastic containter in front of her like a shield. She peered around it with huge, global eyes, looking up into the sky, gazing all around, as if something might swoop down on her at any moment.

"That thing attacked me!" she gasped. "It came right for my face! If I hadn't had this plastic containter and bonked him in the head, it would've got me, for sure."

So, I thought, that explains the loud thwaking sound.

I looked around, but I saw no sign of the beetle.

"Was that the beetle you caught last night?" I asked.

"I don't know," Lindsay said, warily getting to her feet. "I mean, I guess I can't be sure. I think so. I didn't get a good look at him. But it probably was."

"Man!" I said. "That thing was huge! He had wings the size of a sparrow's and pinchers the size of paring knives."

"They're probably just as sharp, too,"

Lindsay said. "That's probably how he sliced and chewed his way out of the box last night."

Lindsay and I continued looking for the insect. We cocked our heads back, searching the sky above and around us. We saw a few birds riding air currents in large, sweeping circles, but other than that, there wasn't anything to see besides the normal things in our neighborhood. A car cruised by, and then another. A guy wearing blue shorts and a yellow shirt jogged along the sidewalk, his rubber soles making muffled tapping sounds on the cement.

"That's a bummer," I said. "I would've liked to have caught that bug and put him in a jar to look at for a while."

"Yeah," Lindsay said, "but you weren't the one who got attacked by him. I really don't care if I never see him again in my life."

"Well," I said, putting my hands on my hips, "we probably won't. He's probably gone for good."

I knew it was silly, but I felt a little sad. I knew that the chances of ever seeing the beetle again weren't very good and that the only picture I had of the insect would be the images in my memory. That would have to be good enough.

But then I had another thought.

"Why don't we see if we can find out what kind of beetle he was?" I said. "I'll bet we could find something on the computer or maybe down at the library."

"I have a better idea," Lindsay said. "My cousin is studying to be an entomologist, and I'll bet she would be able to tell us what kind of beetle it was."

I frowned and scratched my head.

"An ento . . . what?" I asked.

"An entomologist," Lindsay replied as if I should know exactly what the word meant. "Hunter, you of all people should know what that is. I mean, you know all sorts of those weird Latin names for bugs."

I felt a bit silly. Lindsay was right: I probably should have known what the word meant, especially if it had something to do with insects. But I had to admit I'd never heard the term before.

"An entomologist is someone who studies insects," said Lindsay. "My cousin, Joanna, started college to study infectious diseases. She was going to be a doctor. But she's been in love with insects since she was a kid. So, she changed her major, and now she's going to college to study bugs. She's a lot like you: she's fascinated by insects, catches them all the time, and knows all of those funny names."

I was still puzzled. "But then what?" I asked. "I mean, you can go to college to study bugs, but what is she going to do after that? Where does she get a job where someone will pay her to study bugs?"

Lindsay shrugged. "Beats me," she replied. "But we can ask her, if you want. It's Saturday, so she's probably home. Wanna go talk to her?"

"Sure," I said, shrugging my shoulders, not realizing that our trip to visit her cousin would uncover a terrifying secret—a secret that would put our lives in danger. But more than that, it was a secret that would threaten not only Raleigh, but the entire state of North Carolina, America, and even the entire world.

I went home to tell Mom what Lindsay and I had planned. Unfortunately, Mom had her own ideas.

"You can go . . . after you get your room cleaned up," she said.

"Aw, Mom!" I protested, gently stamping my foot, tilting my head to the side, and rolling my eyes. "That's going to take forever!"

Mom shook her head. "I've been telling you all week to do it," she said. "I made Shaina and Abby clean their rooms before going to the park."

"Yeah, but—"

"—yeah but nothing," Mom interjected.

"You're not going anywhere until your room gets picked up. It looks like a pig's sty."

I hate it when she says that. Whenever my room is messy, Mom says it looks like a pig's sty. I don't think she's ever even seen a pig's sty in real life. And besides: my room isn't that messy. Sure, I don't always put my clothes away, and my books and comics are spread out all over the floor, and it looks like a bomb exploded in my closet, but what's the big deal?

Still, it was pointless arguing with Mom. It would just make her mad, and then she would make me stay in the house, and I wouldn't get to go anywhere.

"And another thing," Mom said as I walked down the hall toward my bedroom. I stopped and turned to see my mom glaring at me inquisitively, her hands on her hips.

"What?"

"Your father wants to know how the yard got dug up," she said. "He went to get the newspaper this morning and saw the dirt, and he wonders what you did."

"I didn't do anything, honest!" I said, shaking my head. "I saw that this morning, too."

I was about to explain to her that I thought the mysterious beetle might have something to do with it, but I stopped myself before I spoke. After all, I really didn't have any proof that the insect did anything of the sort. Yes, I saw the beetle fly away from my window last night, and I thought it landed in the yard. But that doesn't mean that it dug up the lawn.

"It doesn't matter," Mom said. "But your father was pretty upset about it. He wants you to cover the hole with something. He's worried about a dog digging it up even more. He'll pick up some sod from the gardening store on his way home. But in the meantime, he wants you to put something over it."

So, there was another thing that I had to do before I met up with Lindsay.

I got to work in my bedroom. It really didn't take all that long, but I kept getting distracted by my comics and books. As I was putting them away, I would flip one of them open and start reading. Soon, fifteen minutes had gone by. Then, after realizing how much time had passed, I would close the comic or the book and hastily put it away, only to do the same thing with another one.

If I keep doing this, I thought, I'm never going to get out of here. I'm never going to get this done.

Finally, just before lunchtime, I finished cleaning my bedroom. Mom made me a couple of sandwiches, and I wolfed them down. Then, I went out to the garage to look for a piece of cardboard or a slab of wood to cover the disturbance on the lawn.

And 'disturbance' was a good word. It wasn't really a hole, and it wasn't really a mound. It was almost as if something had come by in the middle of the night and cut away a piece of the lawn and taken it. Yes, there was a mound of dirt in its place, but there really wasn't a hole there. Not that I could see, anyway.

But when I went out into the yard, all that had changed. I was about to find a lot more than just a simple disturbance in the grass.

In the garage, I didn't have any trouble finding a large chunk of cardboard that was big enough to cover the hole in the yard. Carrying it under my arm, I walked across the driveway and into the daylight. It was still cloudy, but it no longer looked like it was going to rain.

By now, the entire neighborhood was awake. The hum on the distant highway was constant and droning, like a hive filled with busy, mechanical bees. Trees shivered in the light breeze. A few blocks away, a dog barked.

And up ahead, in the yard, was the hole I

had discovered earlier in the day, the small covering of dirt that I'd found that morning.

But I really wasn't thinking about it. The only thing I was thinking was that I was going to put the cardboard on top of it and put a rock on top of the cardboard, and then I would be done with my chores for the day. After I finished, I planned on going to Lindsay's. Her mom was going to drive us over to her cousin Joanna's while she went shopping. Then, she'd pick us up later in the day.

And I'll admit I was a little excited to meet someone who was studying to be an entomologist. Until Lindsay had brought up the word, I never knew a profession like that existed. But the more I thought of it, the more sense it made. I imagined that lots of people study bugs, just the way other people study medicine, rocks, fossils, trees, flowers, or whatever. While I was cleaning my room, I even thought that it might be cool to be an entomologist myself. I was excited to meet Lindsay's cousin and find out more about the study of insects. In fact, while I was cleaning my room, I came across a book I'd recently read about giant, man-eating crickets in Colorado. They were gargantuan, and even though the book was fiction, it scared me so badly I had to sleep with the light on for three nights in a row. I sure wouldn't want to meet up with giant crickets in real life.

I approached the small mound of dirt and knelt down in the grass. Raising the piece of cardboard in front of me, I was about to place it over the dirt . . . when I noticed something odd. Something I hadn't seen earlier that morning.

I leaned in for a closer look. Sure enough, it looked like there were tracks in the clumps of earth, little claw marks that crisscrossed the darkened grains of sand.

Were those there before? I wondered. No. I'm sure of it. If they were, I would've spotted them.

Of course, the first thing that came to my mind was that beetle. The one I had spotted on my window screen the night before.

"I'll bet that beetle caused this," I said out loud, and, suddenly, my mind was filled with images of the insect flying away from my screen last night. I thought about the enormous beetle—or whatever it was—that Lindsay and I had discovered in her garage and how it had attacked her.

But had it really attacked her? I wondered. Did it really attack her, or was she simply in its path of flight? Lindsay seemed to think that the insect tried to get her, and if she hadn't deflected it away with the box, she was sure it would have hit her in the face . . . or worse.

Either way, none of that mattered now. I was sure that Lindsay's cousin, Joanna, would have some answers. I was sure we would be able to describe the insect to her, and, most likely, she would know exactly what kind of bug it was. She would probably be able to tell us all about it, what its name was, what it ate, and if it was dangerous or not.

I dropped the piece of cardboard over the dirt, covering it completely. Then, I looked around.

I didn't see any rocks or anything to place on top of the cardboard, and I thought about leaving it the way it was.

No, I thought, I'd better not. The wind will pick it up and blow it away. I better find something to hold it down.

I stood, turned, and walked back to the garage. On a shelf, I found something that would be perfect: a small can of white paint. Dad and Mom used it when they were painting the trim around the house last summer, and there was still some paint left. It was about the size of a soup can and the perfect weight. I was confident that I could place it on the cardboard without having to worry about the wind blowing it away.

I hustled across the driveway carrying the can of paint with both hands. When I reached the grass, I froze.

Suddenly, I dropped the can of paint onto the ground, not even aware that the lid had popped off and spilled creamy, white liquid all over the green grass. I wasn't aware of the cars and trucks going by on the freeway in the distance. I didn't hear the birds chirping in the trees or the wind slithering through the branches. I noticed none of these things, as I was too shocked by what I was seeing on the lawn.

Ahead of me, only a few feet away, the cardboard that I'd placed over the dirt was moving. It was moving, being pulled into the earth, like somebody—or something—was in the ground, eating it!

12

My body—and my mind—seemed trapped in time. My entire being from my head to my toes was motionless, and my thoughts and mental focus were on one thing:

The vanishing piece of cardboard in the yard.

While I watched, the cardboard slowly crinkled and crunched, the way someone might ball up a sheet of paper in their hand. The only difference was the cardboard was making no sound as it slowly bent and twisted, sinking into the disturbed earth. In only a few seconds, the cardboard had vanished, leaving only a small pile of soft, ruddy earth in the middle of the yard.

Often, when people get really scared, they talk about how a chill races up or down their spine, how the hair on their arms, legs, or back of their necks tends to stand up.

But that's not what happened to me. While I stood there, staring at the dirt, wondering what I had witnessed, a slow, steamy heat crept across my skin. A drop of sweat formed at my right temple and dribbled over my cheekbone, down to my jaw, and to my chin. Slowly, I wiped it away with the back of my hand, never taking my eyes off the space of dirt in the yard.

Is there something in the ground? I wondered. Is there something hidden, unseen, waiting just beneath the surface, hiding beneath the grass?

Of course, lots of things live in the ground. Worms, moles, all sorts of bugs. Ground squirrels, shrews, snakes, lizards.

But none of those things eat big chunks of cardboard, I thought.

It was totally crazy. Completely insane. Nothing I could imagine would cause the cardboard to get pulled into the ground like it had. No animal or insect that I knew of would do something like that.

Cautiously, ever so slowly, I took a step forward. Then another. And another. Soon, I was standing over the disturbed earth, looking at the fresh ground, at the place where the cardboard had been only moments before.

There was no sign of it. Not only that, but the mysterious tracks I had spotted just a few minutes before had vanished. Some of the dirt looked damp and fresh, as if it had been just turned up moments ago.

The warm horror glossing my skin sank into my flesh. I looked around the neighborhood, and I suddenly had the feeling that I was starring in some sort of weird television show, like I was the main character . . . and something very bad was about to happen.

And as it turned out, I was right.

Oh, I wasn't part of a television show. I wasn't in a movie or anything like that. Not by a long shot.

But something really bad was about to happen, and it all came about because I got a stupid idea to try a silly experiment. A silly experiment . . . that I should have never tried in the first place.

13

For whatever reason—don't ask me why—I wondered something:

If I put something else on top of the dirt, would it get sucked into the ground, too?

Still standing over the disturbed earth, I glanced to my right, toward our house. There were several dead branches on the shrubs beneath my bedroom window, and I knew I could break one off easily enough.

Would the dead branch get sucked into the ground like the cardboard?

There was only one way to find out.

I backed away from the hole and then turned and hurried to the bushes. I found a dead branch that was about a foot long, snapped it off, and carried it to the area of disturbed earth. Being careful not to get too close, I reached my arm out and let the stick drop. It landed soundlessly on the dirt.

I waited.

I watched.

A breeze curled around my face, cooling my skin. I realized that my whole body had now broken out with a filmy perspiration, and my shirt felt clammy and sticky. A bead of sweat seeped into my left eye, and it stung.

I squinted, winced, and wiped the back of my hand against my eye to dry my sweat.

Below me, the dead branch stirred. The dirt trembled. Another drop of perspiration brought fire to my right eye, but I ignored it.

The branch was being sucked into the dirt! It was as if it was being eaten by the ground!

I stepped back, just to be safe. I had no idea what was pulling the stick into the ground, and I was worried I might be standing too close.

There was a sharp, cracking sound, and the

branch snapped in two and vanished into the ground. The dirt settled and stopped moving.

And that eerie feeling came over me again, that feeling that I was starring in some movie or I'd become the main character in a bizarre horror novel. Although the day seemed perfect—sunshine, blue skies, birds chirping, a warm breeze, everything you'd expect on a summer day in Raleigh, North Carolina—there was something very, very different about that particular moment.

Something very, very wrong.

I wondered what to do. Of course, the best thing to do was to tell Mom.

But would she believe me?

Probably not.

I would have to show her myself. She would have to see something disappear for herself before she believed me.

But I was still curious. What was causing the items to vanish? What was in the ground that had pulled the cardboard and the stick into the dirt? A creature of some sort?

I also thought about digging into the hole a little. I could use a shovel from the garage and see if I could find whatever was in the ground. But something inside me didn't want to do that. Maybe it was because, deep down, I was afraid of what I might find.

And so, instead of going into the house to get Mom, I decided on one more try.

I turned and spotted the small can of paint that had spilled in the grass. Slowly, I backed up, keeping my eyes on the hole in the ground, but glancing back at the can. Finally, when I reached it, I knelt down and picked it up. I carried it to the disturbed earth, held it out cautiously, paused . . . and dropped it onto the exposed dirt. It landed sideways, like a fat, white ship on a choppy, brown pond, surrounded by a field of soft green blades of grass.

Within seconds, the can began to sink into the dirt! It was being swallowed by some sort of unsen mouth beneath the ground, something under my feet, buried below the carpet of soft grass!

I knelt down, reached out, and grabbed the can, attempting to pull it out before it vanished, hoping to see whatever it was that was sucking it into the ground.

But before I could snatch the can away, a

dark, jagged claw thrust up from the dirt! It latched onto my wrist and began to pull, yanking my hand into the ground!

I don't normally scream, but I found myself crying out louder than I ever had in my life! The shock, horror, and surprise I felt exploded into a high-pitched wail, forced from my gut and out my windpipe. The grip on my wrist wasn't all that painful, but the force yanking me into the ground was terrifying.

I fought with every ounce of strength that I had, using every muscle I could. I tried to pull back, to draw myself away, to free my hand from the clutches of whatever beast was trying to draw me into its lair. My entire right hand was now buried in the dirt, and I could no longer see the claw that clenched my wrist. And I was still screaming at the top of my lungs, shrieking like Shaina or Abby when they saw a spider. Louder, even.

Suddenly, the claw let go. I lost my balance and fell backward, tumbling into the grass. I stopped screaming and heard a screen door bang shut.

"What's wrong?!?!" I heard Mom hollering. She sounded panicked.

I rolled to my side to see my mom rushing toward me, her phone in one hand and a hardcover book in the other. Her face was a mask of dread and confusion.

"What's the matter?!?!"

By then, I had rolled to my knees and stood. I glanced down at my wrist, thankful that I didn't see any blood. There wasn't even a scratch, just a thin, puffy, red welt from where the claw had snared me.

Mom dropped her book and phone on the grass and knelt down in front of me. She placed her hands on my shoulders, and her eyes scanned me up and down from head to toe. Her face was tight and tense, cheeks drawn, eyes narrowed and concerned, pupils darting back and forth as she examined me.

"What's wrong?" she asked. "Why were you screaming?"

My uninjured hand flew out, and I pointed to the mound of dirt.

"That!" I said. "There's something in there! There's something in the ground! It grabbed me and tried to pull me down! It almost sucked me into the ground!"

I held up my other hand, displaying the red welt on my wrist. She took a quick glance at it and dismissed it without question. She glanced down at the disturbed earth and then looked warily at me.

"I've told you a million times not to exaggerate," she said, frowning. She released my shoulders and pointed at me with an accusing finger. The concern in her face melted, and she looked at me sternly. "You can't scream like that. People will think something's wrong."

"But something was wrong!" I insisted. "Something grabbed the can, and then it grabbed my hand. Honest!"

"What can?" Mom asked.

"It was right there!" I said, pointing. "I dropped a stick on the dirt, and it got sucked into the ground. Then, I dropped the empty paint can in the same spot, and it got pulled into the ground, too!"

Mom's eyes narrowed, and her forehead became a roadmap of horizontal lines. I could tell she didn't believe me.

"I'm serious!" I begged, thrusting my finger at the ground. "I saw a claw! That's what grabbed me by the wrist!"

"I'm going to take those scary books away from you," Mom scolded. "If this is what they do to your brain, maybe it's not good for you to be reading them."

"It's not my imagination!" I insisted.

But no matter what I said, Mom wouldn't believe me.

"If I hear you yelling like that again," Mom said, "you're going to be staying in the house the rest of the weekend."

And with that, she hustled back to the house, carrying her book and her phone.

I stared at the dirt mound for a long time, but I didn't get any closer. When the sun went behind a cloud, the ominous shadow painted a sinister, dark cast over the neighborhood. Although nothing had really changed, not really, there was something in my mind—a voice of some sort—telling me that everything had changed. That inner voice we all have was speaking to me from deep within my head, warning me, telling me that something was really wrong, that danger was coming like a freight train, chugging along the tracks at its own unstoppable, comfortable pace, moving solidly and steadily on evil tracks, toward our neighborhood, our street, our house. I could feel that dark freight train of disaster with its smokestack of destruction trailing a thick, boiling black cloud as it moved ever so closer, closer, chugging along, steaming and churning along worn steel tracks, toward—

Me.

A sinister train of horror was coming to Raleigh, North Carolina . . . and there wasn't a thing anyone could do to stop it.

Later that day:

"Bye, Mom," Lindsay called out. "See you later."

We both slipped out of the blue van.

"I'll pick you up in a couple of hours," Lindsay's mother said with a smile. "Don't get into trouble."

"We won't," Lindsay replied, rolling her eyes. She closed the passenger door, and Lindsay's mother drove off, leaving us standing in the driveway of her cousin's house on Dargan Hills Drive. Actually, it wasn't her house, but a place she rented with two other college roommates. It was far outside of the city, about twenty-five minutes from our neighborhood.

In the car, I'd told Lindsay about the stick that had vanished in our yard. I told her about the can that I had placed on the dirt and how a claw had grabbed my wrist.

"So," Lindsay said to me as we stood in the driveway. "What happened after your mom yelled at you?"

"Nothing," I said with a shrug.

"Didn't you try to see what was in the ground?" Lindsay asked, and she started walking up the driveway toward the house.

I stepped alongside her, shaking my head as I spoke.

"No," I said. "I mean, what was I going to do? Stick my hand down there again and let it grab me? I don't think so."

"It must be some sort of bug," Lindsay said. "Maybe it's got something to do with the beetle you saw and the one I caught. I'm sure my cousin Joanna will know what it is."

We climbed the porch, and Lindsay pressed the doorbell. We waited and listened.

Lindsay pressed the doorbell again. We could hear the faint ringing of chimes from somewhere in the house, but that was all. No shuffling feet, no voices, nothing. No one came to the door.

"Are you sure she's home?" I asked.

"I'm sure she is," Lindsay replied. "I talked to her on the phone just a little while ago."

She pressed the doorbell once more, and the chimes bleated again, sounding lonely and muffled within the house. We waited.

Still, nobody came to the door.

"I don't understand," Lindsay said. "I just talked to her. She said she was here, at home."

Lindsay tried the doorknob, and the door creaked open a tiny bit. She pushed it until there was a space of about four inches. Then, she leaned closer.

"Joanna?" she called into the house. "It's cousin Lindsay and my friend, Hunter Freebury. Are you home?"

The house remained silent.

"Doesn't sound like anyone's home," I said quietly.

Lindsay pushed the door open and took a

single step inside. "Joanna? It's me. And Hunter. We're here."

She looked around, taking another step into the house.

"Come on," she said. "She's got to be here somewhere."

I followed her through the living room, which was a mess. There were college textbooks and papers and notes all over the place. A half-full bottle of cola sat on a table, along with an empty, plastic tray of cookies. On the floor was a wadded-up bag of potato chips.

"Wow," I said quietly. "Doesn't your cousin ever clean things up around here?"

"She lives with two roommates," Joanna said. "I'm sure they're all busy with their college studies."

We strode into the kitchen, and the mess was even worse.

Man, I thought. This place looks like a pig's sty.

Then, I smiled. I realized that I was thinking the exact same thing my mom would have thought. She would have called the place a pig's sty.

Lindsay walked to a window. Suddenly, her hands flew up to her mouth. At the same time, she drew in a deep, loud gasp.

"What?" I asked, stepping toward her. I looked out the window.

In the backyard was the body of a woman. She was laying face down in the grass, motionless. Her arms were splayed out, her hands were palms down on the ground by her head. She was wearing blue shorts and a white blouse . . . with a large, red stain of blood on the back!

16

For a moment, we just stood in the kitchen, staring out the window, trying to process exactly what we were seeing. Most obviously, Lindsay's cousin was dead . . . or at least that's what it looked like. She was on her stomach in the grass, she wasn't moving . . . and there was a large blotch of blood staining the back of her shirt.

It was as if time had stopped. I don't remember breathing, and I didn't move a single muscle. Lindsay, too, remained motionless. All we could do was stare.

Suddenly, as if an invisible alarm clock rang,

we snapped out of our trances. Lindsay sprang through the kitchen and around a corner, and I followed. We scrambled through a small alcove that contained a wooden bench, a rug, some shoes, and a door. The door opened into the backyard. Lindsay kicked a black shoe that was in the middle of the floor, and it went flying, ricocheting off the wall and bouncing several times before it came to rest upside down on the floor.

Lindsay turned the knob and threw the door open. She bounded outside, screaming.

"Joanna! Joanna!" she cried. "Are you all right?!?!"

Amazingly, Joanna slowly lifted her head. She drew in her arms, propped herself up on her elbows, and looked at us. Her short, black hair cupped her tanned face.

"Hey, guys," she said calmly. "What's up?"

Lindsay and I slowed as we reached her, and, suddenly, I felt very silly. The red stain on the back of her shirt wasn't blood, after all! It was a rose print! The flower was in bloom, and it was a deep, dark red. From the kitchen, it had only looked like a blood stain on her shirt.

"We . . . we thought you were hurt," Lindsay

said. "We thought that—"

"Thought what?" Joanna asked. She rolled to her side and then glanced down at the grass. "I was just looking at this big beetle here," she said. "I've never seen anything like it. Did you say you thought I was hurt?"

"Never mind," Lindsay replied. I knew that she felt just as silly as I did, thinking that the rose on her cousin's shirt had been a blood stain. Still, I think anyone else would've thought the same thing.

"What kind of beetle did you find?" I asked.

"I'm not really sure," Joanna replied. "I'm not familiar with it. He's not in any of my books, and I've been searching all morning."

I took a few steps closer and knelt down in the grass next to her.

"Where is it?" I asked.

Joanna pointed to a spot in the grass as Lindsay fell to her knees beside me. The three of us leaned forward, peering into the thick, leafy blades.

"He's right there," Joanna said.

At first, I didn't see it. My gaze wandered back and forth, searching, until I finally spotted the bug.

My eyes widened. "That's it!" I said. "That's the same kind of beetle I saw last night at my window!"

Lindsay had spotted the insect and pointed. "And that's the same kind of bug I caught in our garage last night!" she said. "Except the one that I caught was a lot bigger."

"I've seen a few of them," Joanna said. "This morning, there were a couple of them on my window screen. Some were bigger, some were smaller. They flew off when I got closer. I saw this one land in the grass. It took me a few minutes to find him."

We watched the beetle, motionless in the grass. He was mostly black but had brown markings on his back and brown circles around his legs. He was about the size of a quarter.

"And you have no idea what kind he is?" Lindsay asked.

Joanna shook her head. "I've spent all morning looking through books and searching the Internet," she replied. "I haven't found it. The strange thing is that the bigger ones appear to be changing. They still look like the same beetle, but it's like they're growing claws and longer wings."

"Like the one I saw at Lindsay's this morning!" I exclaimed. "It had long claws and wings like a bat."

Joanna nodded. "They're weird, all right," she said. "I have no idea what they are."

"Maybe it's a new species of bug that no one's ever discovered!" I said excitedly. "Maybe we're the first ones to see it!"

"Maybe," said Joanna, "but I kind of doubt it. I'm sure that—"

Joanna was interrupted by a buzzing sound. At first, it seemed far away, but it became louder and louder by the second. It sounded like—

"What's that?" Lindsay asked, turning her head and searching the sky.

Joanna spoke. "It sounds like—"

"—like flapping wings," I said, finishing her sentence.

At that moment, a dark form swooped over the roof of Joanna's house. At first, I thought it was a bird, simply because it was so big. But the three of us quickly realized that it wasn't a bird at all. The flying creature dove down toward us, and even though it didn't get very close, we all ducked as it passed over our heads.

"That was—that was one of them!" Joanna said in disbelief.

"He was gargantuan!" I said.

"He was a monster!" Lindsay cried.

For a moment, I was puzzled about why Lindsay had used that word.

Monster.

I'd never heard that word used to describe an insect before.

Monster.

It was a word for science fiction or fantasy movies, a word used to describe something hideous and threatening. Normally, you wouldn't label any sort of insect with that word.

Monster.

And yet, Lindsay was right. What we were about to discover weren't ordinary insects . . . they were monsters. Hideous creatures from the ground and the sky, unearthly creatures that prowled at night, during the cloak of darkness, searching for unsuspecting victims.

The three of us sat in the grass, looking off into the distance, gazing in the direction in which the insect had vanished. The sun shined down, birds chirped, and a light wind rustled leaves in the nearby trees. In the distance, a car horn honked twice.

"I say we go find him," Joanna said, getting to her feet. Lindsay and I stood, too. Joanna was quite a bit taller than we were, as she was nineteen years old.

"Maybe we can catch him," Lindsay said.

"I hope so," Joanna said.

"And then what?" I asked. While I was excited about the idea of finding and catching one of the bugs, I was a little nervous . . . especially after we'd seen what one of them had done to the box.

"Well," Joanna said, "we'll put him in a jar and find out what kind he is."

"Lindsay caught one of those last night," I said, "and the thing chewed through the box."

Lindsay explained to her cousin how she had caught the giant beetle and how she had put it in a shoe box and left the box in the garage on the floor. She told Joanna how we'd discovered the box this morning, all mangled and torn to shreds. Joanna listened, fascinated.

"I wonder if it's an invasion of a non-native species," she said, her eyes scanning the sky.

Lindsay and I looked at each other. I could tell by the expression on her face that she had no idea what Joanna had meant, either.

"An invasion of what?" I asked.

"A non-native species," Joanna replied. "That's what happens when there is a certain type of animal or insect found in an area where it doesn't usually live. Maybe this type of beetle came from somewhere else in the country. Or maybe a completely different country."

She knelt in the grass. "Let's catch one and take it inside. You guys can help me search on the computer, and we'll see if we can find out what type of insect it is."

Joanna turned her head from side to side, sweeping her gaze across the grass.

"Funny," she said. "It was here just a minute ago."

Lindsay and I knelt down to help Joanna look for the insect. Unfortunately, we didn't find it.

But we did find something else:

A mound of dirt, very small, that had just been unearthed.

"It looks like the beetle dug a hole," Joanna said. She pawed at the dirt, digging a little bit with her fingers.

"That looks just like the mound of dirt I found in our yard!" I exclaimed, pointing. I told Joanna how I'd discovered the mound and how something in the ground had grabbed my wrist. She looked like she didn't believe me.

"Do you think it burrowed into the ground?" Lindsay asked.

Joanna shook her head. "I don't know," she replied. "But I think he's gone."

Suddenly, and without any warning, another insect buzzed above us in the sky. This one was nearly as big as the first one that had flown past. And before we could say anything, another insect flew by. Followed by another. They disappeared into the forest at the edge of the backyard.

"They all seem to be headed in the same direction," Lindsay said.

Joanna nodded. "You're right, Lindsay," she said. "I wonder if they have a nest somewhere in the woods."

"You mean like a hornet's nest?" I asked.

"Exactly," Joanna replied, nodding. "I'll bet if we hunt for it, it won't be too difficult to find."

Have you ever had that voice inside of you that tells you something is really wrong? That little whisper that says danger over and over again? Well, that's what I was hearing in my head. There was something telling me that if we went into the woods, if we sought out the insects, something really bad would happen.

So, what did I do?

I ignored it. I ignored the voice in my head.

I pushed it away and told myself that it was silly, that we were just going to go into the woods and look for some bugs.

Now, I've learned my lesson. Whenever that voice tells me that something is wrong, I listen. I listen, and I obey.

But not this time. This time, I ignored the voice. I pushed it away, thinking I would be safe with Lindsay. And, especially, I would be safe with Joanna, because she was a lot older. She was smarter. She would be able to keep us all safe.

Unfortunately, that wasn't going to be the case. The three of us were headed for the deepest, darkest trouble that we could have ever imagined.

18

"Do you think we'll be able to catch any of them?" Lindsay asked. We were standing in the backyard, just the two of us, while Joanna ran into her house to retrieve her phone.

I shrugged. "I don't know," I said. "Maybe. Especially if we find some big ones."

We heard the back door slam and turned to see Joanna hustling toward us. She was carrying her phone in her left hand, and in her right was a large butterfly net. It had a long, yellow handle and a wide scoop with white mesh netting. I had one just like it, only mine was a lot smaller.

Tucked beneath her left arm was an empty mayonnaise jar with a lid.

Right away, I discovered a problem.

"That net's not going to work," I said, shaking my head and pointing. "The beetle Lindsay caught ripped apart a cardboard box. It'll tear that net to shreds."

"That's what I've got the jar for," Joanna said. "And—"

She stopped a few feet in front of us, put the net down, shoved her phone into her front pocket, and pulled a pair of old leather gloves from her back pocket. "Just in case," she said, giving the gloves a gentle wave. "I figure that if we can catch one in the net, I might be able to grab him and put him in the jar before he tears a hole and gets away. I don't think he'll be able to chew through leather gloves."

"Good thinking," Lindsay said.

Joanna returned the gloves to her back pocket, knelt, and picked up the net. Then, she looked around, like she was expecting to see something.

"What?" Lindsay asked.

"Oh, there's a skunk that's been living under

our front porch over the spring and summer," she said. "He usually comes out only at night, but once in a while, he shows up during the day."

"Can't you get a live trap?" I asked. "You know . . . catch him and release him somewhere else?"

"We might have to," Joanna said, giving the backyard a final glance. "Last night I came home, and he was on the front step of the porch. I'm lucky he didn't spray me."

"We're lucky, too," Lindsay said, holding her nose.

We all laughed at that.

"Ready to head out?" Joanna asked.

We were.

As the three of us started toward the woods, I was bristling with excitement. I've always been fascinated by bugs and beetles and creepy-crawly things, and the thought of discovering some sort of new, unknown insect was thrilling. We'd already seen several of the mysterious beetles, and their sheer size alone was enough to make me want to catch one and inspect it more closely. The jar that Joanna brought would be perfect, as it would contain the bug in glass, allowing us to get a better look without the danger of being bitten or injured by the insect's claws.

Although my family and Lindsay's family lived in residential areas with houses close together, Joanna lived in a more rural area. The homes were farther apart, and there were several large, vacant fields. Directly behind her house, on the other side of a vacant lot, was a thick stand of trees, a large forest without houses or roads. I hoped that Joanna knew where we were going, as I didn't want to get lost in the woods.

But Joanna has her phone, I thought. It probably has a map on it, so we won't get lost, no matter what.

However, as we drew closer and closer to the trees, within the murky shadows beneath the branches, the darkness lurking under the leaves and among the brush and tree trunks seemed unfriendly. Maybe it was just my imagination getting the best of me, but the dark shadows seemed to gnaw at my skin, to eat away at my soul. It was as if the shadows were a warning, an ominous whisper telling us to stay away. Even Lindsay noticed it, because she stopped walking and stared. I stopped, followed by Joanna.

"What?" Joanna asked.

"I don't know," Lindsay replied. Her head turned from side to side as her eyes scanned our surroundings. "But something's not right."

Joanna gazed into the forest that loomed before us.

The shadows whispered ancient, dark poems. The breeze listened and repeated them in hushed, private tones. Branches swayed gently as leaves murmured. Crickets sang from hidden concert halls, and they sounded like rhythmic, jingling coins.

We watched. We listened to the forest's gloomy words of warning.

Finally, Joanna spoke. "It's just a bunch of trees," she said. "It's a forest. There's nothing to worry about."   "It looks kind of dark," Lindsay said warily.

"That's because of the leaves on the trees," Joanna replied confidently. "They block out the sun. Come on. Let's go catch one of those bugs. The three of us are going to be famous."

We started off again. In minutes, we were at the foot of the forest, and Joanna spotted a familiar trail.

"Let's go that way," she said, pointing. "That's a great trail where we ride our bikes. Keep your eyes out for any of those bugs, and I'll keep the net ready. Here." She handed the empty jar to Lindsay. "You hang on to this," she continued, and she grasped the net handle with both hands like a Ninja warrior ready for battle. "Be ready."

She held the net in front of her, and we traveled behind as she followed the trail that led deep into the forest.

The sun vanished as we crept beneath the canopy of thick branches and leaves. There were dapples and splotches of dusty light where a few, crafty rays had been able to sneak through, but mostly, the forest was dark.

And silent.

And moody.

And—

What? I thought. Why am I afraid of the forest? Is it because of the beetles?

I looked around, searching branches and limbs and shadows, looking for anything shiny and black that might be one of the giant insects we were hunting. I noticed, too, that the three of us had knotted together, that we were walking close to one another, and I realized that Lindsay was just as nervous as me. Maybe Joanna was, too, but she was hiding it better because she was older.

So, we remained that way, the three of us huddled closely, walking along the trail in the shadows and darkness of the forest, looking up and around, searching for any sign of the strange insects.

All too late, we realized our mistake. We had been looking up into the branches, searching the limbs and leaves.

We should have been looking down, on the ground . . . because that's where the danger was.

But by the time we realized it, it was already way too late.

19

While we walked, I noticed something else: the temperature had dropped. Not a lot, but enough to chill my skin and cause it to break out in goose-flesh. Most likely, it was because we were no longer in the direct sunlight, but it still felt weird, and my uneasiness only added to the scary feeling I already had.

Every few feet, Joanna would stop. She would freeze and then slowly turn her head, looking around, up and into the trees, in and around shadows. Then, she would start walking again, and we would follow close behind.

"Are you sure you know your way around here?" Lindsay asked quietly.

"Absolutely," Joanna replied, not turning to look at her. "I've been in these woods ever since I was a little kid like you. I know this forest like the back of my hand."

"Hey," Lindsay replied defiantly. "I'm not a little kid."

"Neither am I," I replied.

"Well, both of you are younger than me," Joanna said. "So, you can both believe me when I tell you that I know where I'm going. All we have to do is—"

Joanna stopped speaking and halted. She froze. Very slowly, with her left hand, she pointed to a spot ahead of us.

"There's one, right up there!" she hissed. "On that tree!"

Carefully, Lindsay and I crept closer to Joanna, trying not to move too fast or step on any twigs that might snap. We stopped, Lindsay on Joanna's left, me on her right, huddled close, peering at the place where she was pointing.

At first, I didn't see anything. But suddenly—

"I see it!" I whispered. My heart was hammering.

"I do, too!" Lindsay said.

The insect was clinging to a tree trunk. And he was big, too! He was easily the size of a softball.

"He doesn't even look like a beetle," Lindsay whispered. "He looks like some sort of bat-mole-bug."

Lindsay was right. The beetle's wings were long and fibrous, and his claws were abnormally large for a creature its size.

"Okay," Joanna whispered. "Here's the plan. I'm going to scoop him up in the net and trap him on the ground. When I do," she continued, "Lindsay, you be ready with the jar."

"What do I do?" I asked.

Joanna thought about this for a moment. Then, with her left hand, she pulled the slim, black phone from her front pocket and handed it to me. "You can take pictures," she said.

"Video?" I asked.

"No," Joanna replied softly. "Still pictures will be clearer and better quality. You know . . . for newspapers, web sites, stuff like that."

I was going to argue that it might be cool to

have a video of her actually catching the insect, but I didn't say anything. It was, after all, Joanna's phone. If she wanted pictures, I would take pictures.

So, with Joanna leading the way, the three of us crept silently forward. Joanna was holding the handle of the net with both hands. Lindsay was carrying the jar in her left hand and the lid in her right. I was holding the phone in front of me, in camera mode, ready to begin taking pictures.

The large beetle began crawling up the tree, and Joanna stopped for a moment. She took a deep breath, and we continued.

The bug wasn't moving very fast on the trunk. We were only a few feet away.

"Get ready," Joanna whispered. "Lindsay, are you ready with the jar?"

Lindsay nodded and spoke. "Yep," she replied.

"Okay, Hunter," Joanna said to me. "Start taking pictures. I'm going to catch the beetle in the net and bring him to the ground. I don't think he'll be able to chew his way out. Not right away, anyway. Lindsay, you get underneath the net with the jar and the lid and force him inside. Got it?"

"Got it," I replied quietly.

"Yeah," Lindsay said.

Joanna lunged forward, swinging the net. It made a whooshing sound as the white mesh swept through the air. The rim of the net came down on the tree trunk—but it was too late. The insect, sensing the attack, had taken hasty flight. It buzzed into the air in a flurry of clacking wings and came to rest on a nearby branch.

"He didn't go far," Joanna said. "Do you guys see him?"

"Yeah," Lindsay said.

"I see him," I answered.

Slowly, Joanna left the trail and cautiously made her way toward the insect. Lindsay and I followed, as small branches and brush scraped at our legs.

The phone I was holding suddenly made a chiming bell sound. A red alert came on the screen.

"Hey," I said to Joanna. "Your phone is about dead. You only have ten percent of the battery left."

"That's enough to get some more pictures," Joanna replied.

And it was. But here's what happened, and

this is how a simple hike into the woods to catch a mysterious beetle turned into an endless nightmare of horror.

The beetle kept eluding Joanna's attempts to catch it in the net. Every time she tried, the insect flew off. Not very far, just far enough so we could see it land on another branch or tree trunk. When Joanna swung with the net, it buzzed off again.

Soon, the battery in Joanna's phone died.

Soon, we'd gone farther into the woods than we'd realized.

Soon, it started to get dark.

Soon, we realized we might be lost . . . but we never realized that we were doing exactly what the insect had wanted.

So, of course, we had no idea we'd been led right into a trap. Oh, the trap wasn't set on purpose. Not for us. But that didn't make it any less dangerous.

Neither myself, Lindsay, nor Joanna paid any attention to how late it was getting. Time seemed to stand still. Or maybe it had slowed to a point where it was unnoticeable. I guess it really didn't matter. The only thing that mattered was that we all realized it at the same moment.

"Gosh," Lindsay said, looking around after the bug had flown off yet again. "It's getting dark fast."

"Hunter," Joanna asked, "what time is it?"

"I have no idea," I replied.

"Well, what's the phone say?"

I handed the phone back to her. "The battery's dead, remember? It died a little while ago. I got some pictures, but they're pretty blurry."

"Rats," she said, stuffing the slim phone into her back pocket. "Now, where did that thing go?"

"Are you sure you want to keep trying to catch it?" Lindsay asked. "I mean, we've been chasing after it for a long time. He keeps getting away."

"I'm going to get him," Joanna said confidently.

"I just wonder why we haven't seen any other beetles," I asked. "Earlier today, we saw a bunch of them, and they were all heading into the woods. They all seem to be gone except for the one we've been following."

"They're probably hiding," Joanna replied. "Come on. I'm going to get him this time. He's over there."

We followed Joanna as she pushed away branches and small tree limbs. Lindsay was behind her, and I followed.

"How can you see it?" I replied. "The sun is going down, and there's not much light."

"I can see his shadow, right there on that

branch," Joanna replied. "I'm going to try one more time. If I don't catch him this time, we'll go home."

Once again, the three of us huddled together as we slowly crept toward the insect. Still, I couldn't see it, but Joanna seemed to know where it was.

"Okay," she said. "Ready?"

"Go ahead," Lindsay replied.

Joanna took one step forward . . . and fell. I don't know if she'd stepped into a hole, or what. One minute she was there, and the next she was falling forward. Thankfully, she had let go of the net and grabbed a low hanging branch, and that's what saved her. She'd stumbled upon some sort of hole in the ground, and she hadn't seen it because she was looking up. Plus, it was getting darker by the second.

"Joanna!" Lindsay shrieked.

"I'm okay! I'm okay!" Joanna replied. "Be careful, or you'll fall in yourself."

By now, Joanna had succeeded in using the branch to pull herself up and out of the hole. She had been very lucky. Although it was dark, the hole looked quite big, big enough for all three of us to fall into.

Lindsay grabbed Joanna's hand, pulling her to safety. The three of us stood in the darkening forest, staring down into the hole in front of us. By now, the sun had set. The sky was a faint gray, providing just enough dusk to see shapes and forms around us. Soon, it would be completely dark, and we wouldn't be able to see anything.

"It almost looks like a grave of some sort," Lindsay said.

She was right. The hole was about the same size as a grave, except we couldn't see how deep it was.

"What do you think made it?" I asked.

"Tough to say," Joanna replied.

"Maybe an animal made it," Lindsay said.

"Most likely," replied Joanna, "but I don't know of any animal that would make a hole like this. Bears make dens . . . but they don't dig holes like this."

We stood in silence for a moment, staring at the dark hole, listening to the sounds of the night around us. Crickets were chiming, but they sounded different from the crickets we heard during the day. The crickets during the day had an altogether different song. During the day, they chimed rhythmically, almost as if in circles. At night, they seesawed, and their chimes seemed to go back and forth, back and forth, like a bow on violin strings.

"Well," Joanna said. "I suppose we'd better get back. Your mom is going to wonder where you are if you don't call her soon. And we can't call her until we get to the house where I can plug in my phone and charge the battery."

Joanna started to move, and branches and twigs snapped and crunched. I saw Lindsay's arm shoot out in the murky darkness, grabbing her cousin's arm.

"Wait a second," Lindsay said. There was cold tension in her voice, a suspicious urgency, a warning. "Do you hear that?"

The three of us stopped, listening. The only thing I heard were crickets.

"I don't hear anything," Joanna said.

"I heard something," Lindsay insisted. "It sounded like—"

Then, all three of us did hear a sound.

A gritty, shuffling sound.

Movement nearby.

More shuffling.

Closer.

Closer still.

"Where is it coming from?" I whispered. My lips were tight, and my voice trembled.

The answer came from directly in front of us. A dark shadow emerged from the hole, up, up, higher still. It loomed over us, an atrocious, formidable shape, blocking out the branches above and what little of the sky we could see. It was something so instantly horrifying, so shocking, that the three of us didn't move.

Whatever the thing was, it stopped. There was silence for a moment, and the only thing we heard were crickets.

Then, we heard more shuffling, heavy shuffling, as two giant wings spread up and out, rising above us, reaching out, embracing the darkness.

21

The feeling of complete terror that swept over me was unlike anything I'd ever felt before. There was nothing that could have prepared me for what I was seeing before us, emerging from the hole in the earth. In mere seconds, the enormous creature—or whatever it was—was towering over the three of us.

For a moment, we didn't move. I tried to scream, but I felt oddly out of breath, like all of the air in my lungs had escaped. I opened my mouth, but no sound came out. And I couldn't breathe in, either. Never in my life had I ever felt so powerless, so helpless.

A branch snapped somewhere nearby. The loud crack broke the spell the three of us had been under. Joanna spun, and I felt the firm grip of one of her hands on my shoulder.

"Let's get out of here!" she cried, shoving Lindsay and me back.

The three of us started running, but it was so dark by now that we had no idea which way to go. We had ventured off the trail, and it was now impossible to see anything except greasy shadows and the silhouettes of branches and leaves. Sharp limbs tore at my face, and leafy fronds brushed my cheeks as I fled.

"This way!" I heard Joanna call out from behind me. I stopped just long enough to turn. Joanna had darted to my right, and Lindsay had followed. I sprinted after them, branches and brush whipping at my legs and bare arms.

I moved as if I were in a dream or nightmare. I've had dreams before, nightmares in which I was being chased by someone. In these dreams, no matter how fast I tried to run, it was like trying to move in sludge. My legs wouldn't work, no matter how hard I tried.

That's what it felt like at that particular moment. Although I was running as fast as I could, it didn't seem like it was fast enough. Something was behind us, something had emerged out of the hole, something awful and terrible, and I didn't know if it was chasing us or not.

And I certainly wasn't going to take the time to turn around and find out! I was sure that if I did, the thing would gobble me up on the spot. Or worse: it would fly off with me and gobble me up later.

Up ahead, I heard a loud, cracking sound. Lindsay screamed, and I saw her shadow plunge to the ground. She'd tripped on something and fallen.

"Lindsay!" I shouted, trying to make out her form in the darkness.

"I'm okay!" she said as she scrambled to her feet.

"Come on!" Joanna urged. She had paused for a moment to turn around to help Lindsay, but now that Lindsay was back up on her own, she didn't need anyone's help.

"Where's the trail?" I shouted.

"It's up here, somewhere!" Joanna replied. "Don't worry! We'll find it!"

We didn't. In fact, the more we ran, the more dense the forest became. It seemed as if the limbs were getting sharper, scratching at my arms and face. A branch struck the lower part of my forehead, tearing at my eyebrow. If it had been an inch lower, it would've hit me directly in the eye.

"Ouch!" Lindsay cried. She stopped in front of me, and I smacked into her, nearly knocking her over. "I just hit something with my knee!"

Ahead of us, Joanna stopped. She turned around, retraced a few steps, and her dark silhouette appeared.

"Are you okay?" she asked.

All three of us were breathing heavily, our chests heaving, gasping for air.

"I think so," Lindsay said. "I hit something with my knee. A stone or something. It hurts bad."

"Listen," I said.

"What?" Joanna asked.

"No, I mean listen. Listen to the sounds."

For the next few seconds, the only thing we could hear were the sounds of our own heavy breathing and crickets. That's it. No other snapping branches, no crunching sounds. No indication that anything was following us.

We waited.

We listened.

Gradually, our breathing became easier. The sounds of the night became more distinct, sharper and clearer. The crescendo of crickets was nearly overwhelming. Somewhere, high above, we heard the lonely drone of an airplane. Also, in the distance, a car horn honked. They were reminders that the real world was still out there, somewhere, around us.

But it was a world, at that moment, that seemed very distant. The forest had become our world, and it was a place very different from what we would have considered the real world. Somehow, we'd traveled to a world of giant bugs, a world of enormous beetles. A world where a mysterious, dark creature had emerged from a hole in the ground. And while I still had no idea who or what it was, something told me that it was really, really bad.

Then, Lindsay spoke. It was the sound of her voice, the tone of her words that sent chills down my spine.

"Um, guys," Lindsay said softly. Her voice trembled. "I hate to tell you this, but look up into the sky."

Slowly, I raised my chin and tilted my head back, gazing into the dark night. Gazing up at the stars that I hadn't known were there until just that moment. Gazing up through skeletal tree branches and odd-shaped leaves.

Gazing up into a new definition of horror.

22

The three of us stared, mesmerized by the sight in the dark sky above us. We could see a great many stars, but some of them were hidden by blotchy, torn clouds.

But we weren't looking at the stars or the clouds.

We were looking at the monstrous form rising above the trees and what seemed like a thousand smaller things swarming around it.

"What is that thing?" Lindsay asked.

"It must be some sort of giant insect," Joanna replied. Her voice carried a mixture of fear, awe, and fascination. As someone who studies insects, I was sure she was captivated by the scene above.

However, she was also frightened. What we were seeing was something so out of the ordinary—so bizarre—and there really was nothing we could do but stare.

"It reminds me of a swarm of bees," I said. "It's like all of the drones are following the queen."

Joanna gasped.

"Hunter!" she said. Her voice was muffled, but filled with excitement. "I'll bet you're right! I'll bet there must be some sort of nest of some sort here in the woods! Maybe it's where that hole in the ground is!"

"But we don't even know what they are," Lindsay said. "All we know is that they're some sort of beetle that we've never seen before."

"And that's not all that out of the ordinary," Joanna said. "Scientists are discovering new species of insects every day. They say there might be thousands of new types of bugs that we've never seen before. Maybe we're seeing one of them."

"Maybe so," I replied. "But since when do bugs grow to the size of humans?"

Joanna didn't have an answer to that. Neither did Lindsay. And so, for the next few minutes, all we did was watch and stare up into the sky.

Slowly, the enormous form circled higher and higher into the dark sky until it was only a single speck, blending in with the murkiness of night. We could no longer see the smaller insects swarming around it.

"And you didn't get any pictures?" Joanna asked me.

I shook my head. "No," I said. "I got some blurry ones before the phone battery died, and that's about it."

"Bummer," Joanna said. "A picture would have helped us identify it. Maybe it's a new species of beetle, maybe it's not."

"Is there anyone that you know that might have a clue?" I asked. "Maybe someone at your college?"

"Possibly," Joanna said. "I can check around. But if I start telling people that I saw a giant, man-sized beetle, they're going to think I've lost my mind."

"At least we're safe," Lindsay said. "At least

that thing is gone. At least—"

And that's when Joanna screamed.

23

If things hadn't already been weird enough, they were about to get a lot weirder.

Joanna's scream startled us. I flinched and stopped walking, my body and mind on full alert, ready to fight or flee, trying to determine the threat that had caused Joanna to scream.

Then, I saw it.

A ghost.

Right in front of us.

Coming toward us!

My heart rammed at my chest in rapid fire, hammering my rib cage. Blood surged through my head, creating a tingly, swirling sensation. My skin felt hot and suddenly clammy as I prepared to turn and run.

"Who's there?" the ghost demanded. Only, it didn't sound like a ghost. It sounded like the muffled voice of a man. A man with a thick, foreign accent. Other than that, I guess he sounded like a normal, everyday man, asking a question—and not a ghost.

We didn't say a word.

"Who's there?" the man asked again in his thick, foreign accent, a little louder this time, and even more demanding. However, his voice sounded hollow and muted, like he was wearing a mask. "I can see someone there. Who are you?"

He'd stopped walking and was only a few feet in front of us now. In the glow of the moon, I could see a bluish-white blob in the shape of a man, but he looked oddly large and misshapen, cartoon-like. Ghost-like.

Lindsay spoke. "It's us," she said, her voice trembling.

"But who are you?" the man said, his voice more insistent. "Where do you live? And why are you here, in the middle of the woods at night?"

He sounded a little angry, but I could also tell that he was surprised, curious, and maybe even a little anxious and tense.

Of course, I had questions of my own. If he was a man, which he was, what was he wearing, and why was he out in the woods in the middle of the night?

"I'm Joanna," Joanna said. "This is my cousin, Lindsay, and her friend, Hunter. They live in the city. I live over on Dargan Hills Drive."

"You shouldn't be out here," the man said. Then, he raised his arms to his face. There was a zipping sound, and he took off a white hood that was connected to his white suit.

"Why?" Joanna asked.

"The beetles," the man replied.

"That's what we've been looking for," I said. "We've been trying to catch one."

"You've been what?!?!" the man exclaimed.

"We've been trying to catch one so we can study it," Joanna said, "but we saw a huge bug and a swarm come up from the ground just a few minutes ago. That's when we got scared."

"You're very lucky," the man said. "It's extremely dangerous out here. How far away do you live?"

"Not far," Joanna said. "But now that it's dark, I guess we're kinda lost."

"Well, you can come with me," the man said, motioning us toward him with his bulky, white arm.

The three of us didn't move. After all, we had no idea who the man was or where he was going to take us.

Sensing our apprehension, he spoke again, introducing himself as Yuri Ivandrovich.

"I am a scientist," he said. "Please. You must come with me. It's not safe here. It is, as you say here in America, a matter of life and death."

In the darkness, Joanna looked at us. I looked at her, and I was glad she was with us. She was older than we were, and I trusted that she had a better sense of the situation.

"Come on," she said. "It'll be okay."

"I'll explain more while we walk," the man said. He fitted his hood over his head and zipped it into place. His voice was now hollow in its containment. "You three are completely unprotected, so we must hurry."

Unprotected? I thought. What does he mean

by that?

I had to admit that just the man's tone of voice had me worried. He sounded serious, like it really was a life or death situation.

And as he began to explain, I realized that it was. At that very moment, walking through the dark forest, we were in a life or death situation.

But for us, what was it going to be: Life . . . or death?

24

"Where are you taking us?" Joanna asked as we followed the white-suited man through the dark forest.

"We've set up a base camp in a field not far from here. It's far enough away from any houses and close to the colony of creatures."

Colony? I thought. Where? In the ground? I had a lot of questions, but, fortunately, Mr. Ivandrovich continued to explain what was going on. He said there was a deadly species of beetle believed to have been extinct years and years ago. But what they found out was that the beetles laid their eggs deep in the ground, where they remained for years.

"Their gestation period is exactly one hundred years," Mr. Ivandrovich explained. "The eggs hatch, and the beetles emerge from the ground. They grow incredibly fast, reaching enormous sizes in just a few short days. They'll eat just about anything."

"Anything?" Lindsay asked.

"Anything," Mr. Ivandrovich restated firmly. "But that's not the problem. The problem is that the beetles carry a variation of a killer bacteria called Yersinia pestis, and—"

Joanna stopped suddenly. She had been walking in front of me, behind the foreign man in the white suit, and I bumped into her. Lindsay was last, and she smacked into me.

"Wait a minute," Joanna said. "I've heard that before. Yersinia pestis. Isn't that—"

"The bacteria that causes the bubonic plague," Mr. Ivandrovich replied gravely. "The bacteria the beetle carries is a slight variation, but the effects are equally devastating. But how did you recognize the name?"

"I was studying infectious diseases in college

for a while," Joanna explained. "I read all about the bubonic plague."

"What's the 'bubonic plague?'" I asked. I'd heard of it before, but I wasn't really all that familiar with it.

"It was a horrible disease in the 1300s," Joanna explained. "It was called the 'Black Death.' It killed millions and millions of people in Europe."

"That's right," Mr. Ivandrovich said. "Some estimates are as high as seventy-five million people."

"Seventy-five million people?!?!" Lindsay said.

"Yes," Mr. Ivandrovich replied. "It wiped out much of Europe's population. But let's keep walking. I'm wearing a protective suit that will keep me from being bitten. Without protective suits, you are all in danger. If you are bitten by one of these beetles, if they break the skin and infect a person, this new strain of bacteria will enter their bloodstream immediately. There is no cure. The disease can travel through the air, and anyone who catches it will help spread it to another, and another, and another. Without a cure, there would be no stopping it."

He didn't have to say anything more. I could tell by the dark, heavy sound of his voice that he was dead serious . . . and that made me even more afraid.

"And to think," Lindsay said, "I caught one of those things in a box because I thought it was cool," she said.

I shuddered when I remembered my hand being grabbed by something when I'd reached into the hole in our yard. I could have been seconds away from being bitten. But the thing hadn't broken my skin; it hadn't bitten me. Still, that didn't make me feel any better.

Mr. Ivandrovich explained that the large insect we'd spotted coming up from the hole in the earth wasn't an insect, after all, but a mechanical drone! The flying robot was created to look like a large insect that reproduced the mating call of the beetle. The theory was that it would attract all of the beetles, and they would follow it to a location not far away where a trap had been set. When the drone landed, the swarm of beetles would follow. A large net would be deployed, capturing all of the beetles and preventing their escape.

"The hole you came across was the one we

dug for the drone. We placed the robot in the ground, where it began broadcasting a subsonic signal to creatures that were still in the earth."

"What's 'subsonic' mean?" Lindsay asked.

"It's a frequency that can't be heard by humans," Mr. Ivandrovich replied. "Only certain animals—and insects—can detect it."

"So it would attract other beetles?" Joanna asked.

"Exactly. You all are very lucky not to have been bitten," Mr. Ivandrovich said. "Actually, up until now, the entire city of Raleigh has been very fortunate, as well as everyone in America. Even the world. But the drone is in the air, the swarm of creatures is moving toward our trap, and I think everyone will be safe. Unless there's a—"

"Ahhhhhghghghgh!" Lindsay shrieked from behind me. "It's on my neck! It's on my neck, and it bit me!"

25

There was a frantic flurry of activity in the darkness. I spun to see Lindsay's ghostly form fall to the ground and roll to the side, both hands clasping her neck. Already, Mr. Ivandrovich was on the move, kneeling over her in his white suit.

"Where is it?!?!" he demanded.

A flashlight in Mr. Ivandrovich's hand clicked on, and the beam was wild and erratic.

"My neck! He got me on my neck!" Lindsay wailed.

The flashlight beam steadied for a moment.

"That wasn't a beetle," Mr. Ivandrovich said

with relief. "That was only a mosquito. And you squished him. You're fine."

Everything seemed to stop for a brief moment, and all we could hear were crickets. Then, Lindsay spoke.

"Oh," she said. "Oh, okay. But he really stung me hard."

"A mosquito?" Joanna said with mild annoyance.

"Hey, it hurt bad," Lindsay said, defensively.

"We're wasting time," Mr. Ivandrovich said, helping Lindsay to her feet. "Let's keep going."

Again, we set out through the woods. It seemed as though Mr. Ivandrovich had picked up the pace, and the rest of us struggled to keep up with him. Branches cracked and snapped beneath our feet, and thin limbs and dry, papery leaves smacked at the bare skin of our arms, necks, and faces.

A radio squawked, and Mr. Ivandrovich stopped, causing the three of us to do the same. Mr. Ivandrovich pulled off a white glove, dug into a pocket, and produced a small radio.

"Ivandrovich," he said, his voice hurried and tense.

After a brief pause, the radio barked to life, static and gritty.

"What's your location, Yuri?" a man's voice said, crackling through the airwaves.

"I think we're about a thousand meters out," he said.

In my head, I calculated how far that would be. Although we don't use the metric system very much in America, we learned all about it in class. A meter is about three feet, so according to Mr. Ivandrovich, we were about 3,300 feet from our destination. And I also knew there were 5,280 feet in one mile, so that would mean we were over a half mile away. That didn't seem like it was very far, but, then again, we were trudging through the forest at night, and we weren't following a trail. It may have seemed like Mr. Ivandrovich had been moving fast, but it was going to take us a few minutes to get where we were going . . . wherever that was.

"We've got the swarm on radar lock," the scratchy voice came again. "It won't be long now."

Mr. Ivandrovich pocketed his radio.

"We've got to hurry," he said to us in the darkness.

Joanna spoke. "But if all of the beetles are gathered in the swarm in the sky," she said, "what do we have to worry about?"

"We can only hope that the mating call has attracted all of the beetles," Mr. Ivandrovich replied. "We don't know for sure. And if we don't know for sure, we must be extra careful."

I didn't really know what he meant by 'extra careful,' as we were completely unprepared. If one of those beetles decided to attack us, we wouldn't even see it coming. There was nothing we could do to stop it.

But I had another question.

"If those bugs have been in the ground for one hundred years," I said, "what happened one hundred years ago? Didn't they come out of the ground and bite people way back then?"

"Yes," Mr. Ivandrovich replied. "However, one hundred years ago, the bacteria was different. The bite of the insect caused illness, but it was mostly flu-like symptoms. Nobody died. We've only recently discovered the variation of the bacteria."

Again, we set out. While we walked, Mr. Ivandrovich went on to explain about how a beetle was discovered, tested in a laboratory, things like that. He used a lot of long words and technical descriptions that I didn't understand.

But I understood one thing: we had to get out of the forest as soon as possible.

Moving through the dark forest, I thought about my parents and how they were probably worried sick. I was sure they were looking for me. Maybe they'd even called the police. I didn't think I'd get into trouble, because what was happening really wasn't our fault. But still, I knew my parents were probably freaked out, and I didn't like to think that I was causing them so much worry.

So, to get my mind off that subject, I tried to calculate my steps in my head, tried to figure out how long it would take to get where we were going.

"Almost there," Mr. Ivandrovich said. "I can see the lights ahead."

In two minutes, we stood at the edge of a large, brightly-lit field. The field was flat and empty, circled by trailers and motor homes and emergency vehicles with whirling and flashing lights. Tall antennas shot high into the sky like lances. It was impossible to see if there were any stars, because the floodlights were so bright that the glare washed out the scene above us.

But below, in the field, the area was lit up like a sunny afternoon.

Mr. Ivandrovich pointed. "Over there," he said, and I followed his finger to a large trailer. "It'll be safe for you there. You'll be able to call your parents."

"My parents are gonna ground me for life," Lindsay said. "They're going to take away all of my games and my phone and my computer. My life is over."

My life is over.

That sentence seemed to hang in the darkness and eat at my flesh.

My life is over.

And I could still hear Lindsay's words in my head as sharp legs and claws dug into my neck and squeezed. I screamed and went to my knees, but the only thing I heard were Lindsay's words in my head, repeating.

My life is over . . . my life is over . . . my life is over . . . .

26

"Take it easy, take it easy!" Mr. Ivandrovich said, nearly shouting in his thick, foreign accent. "It's just me. Sorry about that."

He released his gloved hand from my neck. He hadn't meant anything by it; he was only urging me on in an effort to get me moving. His grasp was meant to be a protective, guiding hand, not a beetle that was about to bite me.

I got to my feet without saying anything.

Suddenly, a siren began to wail. Mr. Ivandrovich's radio sputtered to life in his pocket, and he quickly removed his glove and pulled out the device.

"Ivandrovich," he said gruffly.

"Where are you?!?!" a metallic, frantic voice sputtered from the speaker. "The swarm is coming in!"

The four of us looked up at the same time, searching the glare of the sky, but there was nothing to see.

"We're at the field, on our way to trailer Nine. Ivandrovich out."

He pocketed the radio and put his glove back on, and the four of us hustled across the field in a frenzied run. Even Mr. Ivandrovich moved fast in his white suit, which was now brightly lit in the harsh floodlights. Later, Lindsay would quip that he looked like a giant marshmallow running through the field, and I would laugh out loud. But right now, the only thing we could think of was making it to the safety of the nearest trailer. Our lives were at stake, and there was nothing funny about that.

The siren continued to wail, heightening my sense of urgency. Again, I thought about the beetle at my window the previous night, the mysterious mound of dirt in our yard, and the beetle that

Lindsay had caught. I had no idea how dangerous the situations had been, how close we had been to death.

If one of those things had bitten us, I thought, we wouldn't even be here right now.

While we ran, I kept glancing into the sky, searching for a swarm of insects. However, the glare of lights pouring down was so bright that I couldn't see beyond them. With so many intense bulbs burning, it was like looking up at a dozen suns positioned around the field, illuminating the vehicles and trailers.

But now that we were closer, I could see the field better. In the middle was a large hole, the size you'd make if you were digging a basement for a house. Large piles of dirt were piled up around it, and there were several backhoes and other large machinery parked nearby. It appeared that the hole had been hastily dug, maybe even earlier that afternoon.

We reached the trailer, and Mr. Ivandrovich threw open the door. He stood aside, holding the door open with one hand and sweeping us in with the other. A wave of relief washed over me as I burst into the bright light of the trailer.

We'd made it. We were out of danger, safely out of harm's way. We would be home soon.

At least, that's what I thought.

27

A man and a woman, each wearing white lab coats, were in the trailer. Both looked shocked to see us. It was as if they had been in the middle of something when we burst inside, and they both froze, eyes wide, staring at the four of us as if we were ghosts.

Mr. Ivandrovich closed the door behind us, muting the sound of the wailing siren.

"These three kids were in the forest," Mr. Ivandrovich explained as he slipped the white protective helmet from his head. "I had to bring them with me. I couldn't leave them out there alone."

The man in the trailer relaxed and went about his business at a computer screen in front of him. The woman was also standing in front of a computer, but she continued to glare at us.

"You're very lucky," she scolded in a familiar, average-American voice. "You three could've been in big, big trouble."

"We're going to be," I said, "if we don't call our parents and let them know where we are."

Outside, the siren faded. The man behind the computer suddenly tapped the screen with his finger.

"There's the swarm!" he said. "Right on time and just as we suspected!"

The woman turned her attention to the computer. Mr. Ivandrovich stepped in and peered over her shoulder. I wanted to see, too, and so did Lindsay and Joanna. The three of us shuffled in and tightened into a knot behind the man and woman in lab coats.

There really wasn't anything to see. The computer screen looked like a weather radar monitor that showed the land and terrain from above, only instead of a green blob of rain, this showed a small, black blob of ink. That, of course, was the swarm.

"The beetles are following the drone decoy," the woman said. She glanced up and looked out the window. "This is going to be perfect. When the drone lands in the hole, the beetles will follow. That will be our cue to launch the spring nets."

A radio on a shelf spluttered to life.

"They're coming down," a man's crackling voice said. "Remember: don't launch the nets until the swarm is below ground level."

Our attention turned from the computer monitor to the window and the bright lights positioned around the field. At first, there was nothing to see. Then, Mr. Ivandrovich pointed.

"Right there," he said, his heavy, thick accent filled with fascination. "The drone is coming down, and the swarm is following."

Suddenly, I saw a dark shape, an object about the size of a softball, swoop beneath the bright lights. Then another that was a bit smaller, and another. In seconds, there were hundreds of them—maybe thousands or more—swarming the air above the field. It looked like a tight knot of giant bees, a whirling tornado of insects, slowly lowering to the field. And somewhere, in the middle of that swarm, was the 'dummy' insect, the drone that was masquerading as the queen beetle.

"The drone is entering the hole," the man behind the computer said. "Wait until all of the insects have followed it."

It was a fascinating scene to watch, and quite unbelievable. Again, I reminded myself how lucky we'd been.

The man at the computer snapped up the microphone. "Okay," he said. "Launch the nets!"

From around the field, rockets sprang into the air, pulling a heavy, mesh net. The rockets carried the net over the hole until it fell to the ground. The rockets themselves hit the ground and fizzled out in puffs of smoke.

"Perfect!" Mr. Ivandrovich said. "It's covered the entire hole!"

The net blanketed the hole like a carpet, sinking a bit toward the middle. And it moved, too, as the beetles hit it from beneath. Bumps and bubbles came and went as the insects tried to escape, but couldn't. They were trapped.

In seconds, more people appeared around the hole, emerging from trailers and emergency vehicles.

"It's working," Mr. Ivandrovich said confidently. "We're very fortunate that our plan is succeeding. This will be—"

The radio squawked to life. Outside, the people in the white suits began running back to the trailers and emergency vehicles.

"Everybody back!" a voice from the radio squealed. "They're chewing through the net! They're chewing through the net and escaping!"

28

The six of us in the trailer stared out the window.

"Impossible," the woman said in a voice just above a whisper. "That net is made out of metal micro-fiber. There's no way the insects can chew through it."

The woman was wrong.

A beetle appeared, emerging from a hole in the netting material. It buzzed up toward a light and swooped down again.

The man in front of the computer grabbed the microphone again, speaking into it.

"Keep the drone signaling," he barked.

"Don't turn it off. If it stops sending out that call, the beetles will fly off. We've got to make sure they remain close."

Outside, two people in white suits re-emerged from one of the emergency vehicles. Both were carrying what appeared to be heavy fire extinguishers. Each carried these with one hand, while in the other, they carried a hose connected to the extinguishers.

The beetle that had chewed through the hole made a tight circle in the air and then shot straight at the two men. Both lifted the hoses they were carrying. From one of the hoses came a stream of liquid that shot into the sky. It hit the beetle, and the insect instantly stopped its assault and fell to the ground.

"Most unfortunate," Mr. Ivandrovich said. "I was hoping something like this wouldn't happen."

"What?" Joanna asked.

"The insects are being exterminated," he replied. "I was hoping we could capture them alive for study, but it appears that won't happen. If the beetles are able to escape the net, we have no choice but to destroy them before they become a threat."

"Maybe some of them can be saved," I said.

"I hope so," Mr. Ivandrovich said.

"Does anyone have a phone?" Lindsay asked. "I have to call my mom. She's probably really worried."

The woman at the computer pointed to a black, rectangular phone resting on a table. "You can use that one," she said. "The password to unlock it is 'mittens.' That's the name of my cat."

Lindsay picked up the phone, typed in the password, and punched in her mom's phone number. She backed into a corner of the trailer and began talking to her mom. It was obvious that her mom was frantic. Lindsay was trying to calm her down, telling her that she was fine, that everything was okay.

Meanwhile, the rest of us continued watching the bizarre scene unfolding in the field. A few more beetles had escaped, and more white-suited people had appeared with hoses and canisters of some special bug killer. The escaping beetles didn't have much of a chance.

The man who had been at the computer began chatting on the radio; the woman was frantically typing at her keypad.

Mr. Ivandrovich turned to Joanna.

"You three wait here," he said. "I'll see if it's okay for you to leave. If it is, I'll see if I can arrange for a ride for you. Dargan Hills Drive isn't far away, but it would be best if you had an escort."

He exited the trailer without putting his protective hood over his head, so I figured that the situation was no longer as dangerous as it had been. In a few moments, he returned.

"I think it's all clear," he said.

Lindsay had said good-bye to her mother and offered the phone to me. I had been dreading the call to my parents, because I knew they'd be worried. And I was afraid that I might be in trouble, even though everything that happened hadn't been my fault.

I called my mom, but I was sent to her voicemail. I left her a quick message saying that I was okay, that I would be at Joanna's house very soon. I felt bad because she had no way to call me, because Joanna's phone was dead. But at least she knew I was safe. I knew we weren't too far from Joanna's house, and we would all be home soon. All of the beetles had been captured.

Mr. Ivandrovich returned to the trailer with

a uniformed police officer, who glanced warily at each of us.

"Officer Hubbard has offered to take you three home," he said. "You'll be safe riding with him."

I've never been in a police car, I thought as the three of us left the trailer and stepped into the salty, white haze of the floodlights. But at least we'll be at Joanna's in a few minutes. This whole thing will be over.

And that's what I thought as the three of us climbed into the back seat of the police car, not knowing that there was an awful surprise waiting for us at Joanna's house.

29

It took only a few minutes to get back to Joanna's house on Dargan Hills Drive. We thanked Officer Hubbard as we got out of the patrol car.

"I'll wait here until you guys get inside," he said. He glanced at Lindsay and then at me. "You sure you don't need a ride to your houses?"

"I'm sure," Lindsay said. "We'll just wait here at Joanna's house. My mom is going to be here any minute, and she can take Hunter home."

"Okay, then," the police officer said. "I'll wait here for you, until you're safely inside the house."

Joanna, Lindsay, and I began walking up the driveway. Here, away from the glare of the floodlights and the field, we could see deep into the night sky. It was an enormous canopy of glittering stars, mini-suns that were millions and millions of miles away. Tiny, shining pearls in an ocean of blackness. I'd always been fascinated with stars, galaxies, and planets, and I'd often look up and wonder if there were other forms of life, somewhere out there, in the distant heavens.

Now, however, something else was on my mind. I kept looking for movement, for dark shapes darting through the sky, searching for a beetle zipping through the darkness, a creature carrying a deadly bacteria that could wipe out humanity. It was a terrifying thought.

Lindsay and Joanna, however, had left their fears behind. They were talking and laughing about what had happened, and both seemed pleased that they'd had the adventure, that everything was all right.

"I only wish I'd had the chance to observe one of those things for a little bit longer," Joanna said.

"You're crazy," I said. "If that thing would've

170

bitten you, you'd be dead."

"True," Joanna replied. "But it was still an exciting discovery."

When we reached the porch, I turned. The police car was still parked at the curb, headlights on. In the glow of a distant streetlight, I could see the unlit light bar on top, the faint outline of the police emblem on the door, and the silhouette of Officer Hubbard seated behind the wheel, waiting patiently.

"Let's get inside," Joanna said, pulling out her phone from her back pocket and motioning toward me. "I can plug this in, and you can try calling your mom again."

Joanna put one foot on the first step of the porch and stopped. Then, she leapt back.

"Oh, no!" she screamed. "Run! Run fast!"

30

Once again, my heart and brain were sent into hyperdrive. I wasn't sure what was wrong, why Joanna had suddenly leapt back and screamed, but I was sure she must have spotted a beetle somewhere in the shadows of her porch.

But it wasn't.

Something moved near the door. At first I thought it was a cat, as that was about the size of the creature. But then I realized what it really was, and I, too, leapt back. When I did, my left foot caught my right leg, and I fell, hitting the ground with a thud. I immediately rolled to my side, sprang to my feet, and darted out onto the lawn.

Lindsay, however, was laughing as she ran back.

"What is it?" I heard Officer Hubbard shout as he sprang from his patrol car.

"Skunk!" Joanna shrieked, slowing as she reached the street. "He's been living under the porch all summer, and he was by the front door!"

Officer Hubbard laughed. "Well, it looks like you guys got away just in time. Good thing that's been your worst trouble tonight."

He was right, of course. We'd been very lucky, considering everything that had happened. But in the end, everything turned out okay. Lindsay, Joanna, and I were safe, and we'd been spared the wrath of the horrible beetles, the creatures of the night that could have threatened the lives of every person on Earth. We were safe, Raleigh and the rest of North Carolina was safe, the world had been spared from a horrifying bacteria carried by bugs that had been hibernating in the ground, waiting for their time to be up, waiting for their hundred-year cycle to be complete. The relief I felt was overwhelming.

Unfortunately, my relief wouldn't last long.

31

Thankfully, nothing more happened at Joanna's house. After the skunk waddled off, Officer Hubbard left. After making sure the skunk wasn't hanging around, we went inside. Surprisingly, Joanna's roommate was still sleeping. Even with all the commotion outside, she hadn't awoke.

"She's a pretty heavy sleeper," Joanna said, not even bothering to whisper. "She can sleep through anything . . . especially her college classes."

I called Mom, and she answered on the first ring. She sounded panicked, but she was happy to hear my voice. She and Dad had been worried, but she said she was glad that I'd called earlier and left her a message. I told her a little bit about the beetle invasion and what had happened, but she hadn't heard anything about it.

Lindsay's mom came and picked us up. We chatted like monkeys all the way to my house, trying to explain what had happened. Lindsay's mom kept glancing at us, wondering if we were telling the truth. I think she thought we were making up the entire story.

My parents, of course, were waiting up for me when I got home. Shaina and Abby were in their rooms, but I caught Shaina peeking out the crack of her bedroom door, trying to listen in as I explained everything that had happened that day. Mom and Dad listened, but they glanced at each other the way Lindsay's mom had looked at us in the car. Like her, they were wondering if I was making up the whole thing.

When I finally went to bed, the last thing I remember was thinking how lucky I'd been. Actually, we'd all been very lucky. If what Mr. Ivandrovich had told us was true, the entire world had escaped what could have been nothing less than total catastrophe. I fell asleep, thankful I was in my bed, in my house, with my family. I was thankful I was alive.

I was awakened in the middle of the night by a scraping against the window screen. At first, the sound was distant, and in my sleepy haze, it sounded like it was coming from the far end of a tunnel, far away. Gradually, as I awoke, the scraping and buzzing became louder and stronger, more intense. Finally, I was wide awake. It took a moment for my eyes to focus, but there was no mistaking what I was seeing: a huge beetle clawing at the screen, trying to get inside!

32

When I saw the huge shadow at my screen, I suddenly remembered the horrifying episode from the day before. I shot up in bed, propped on my elbows, screaming like crazy. I know it sounds silly, that I was overreacting, but that's what happened. Besides: I think anyone else would have done the same thing, if they'd been through the same ordeal I had the day before.

My screams, of course, alerted my parents, and there was a thunder of horses' hooves as my mom and dad came racing down the hall. My bedroom door burst open, and harsh, white light flowered.

"What?!?!" Mom said, rushing to my bedside. "What's wrong?!?! What's the matter?!?!"

I pointed. "That!" I gasped. "That thing! It's trying to get in! Don't let it! Don't let it get inside!"

Shaina and Abby appeared in the doorway, and I realized that this event was the same as the night before: I had awakened screaming, Mom and Dad came, followed by Shaina and Abby.

Dad went to the window and leaned forward, peering at the beetle on the other side of the screen.

"For crying out loud, Hunter," he said. "It's just a June bug."

I scrambled out of bed to see for myself. Sure enough, the insect grasping the wire-mesh screen was just an average, ordinary, everyday June bug. Nothing more.

In the doorway, Shaina and Abby giggled. Mom glared at them. "You two go back to bed. Now."

Reluctantly, Shaina and Abby turned and vanished in the dark hallway.

"I thought it was one of those other beetles," I said with a shudder. "I thought it was one of those . . . those . . . creatures."

"It's nothing to worry about," Mom said. "Go back to sleep."

My parents left my room, and I was alone, feeling a bit sheepish. But then again, I was thankful that the insect at my screen was just an ordinary June bug. I don't know what would have happened, what I would have done if it had been one of those other . . . things.

I must have slept well the rest of the night, because I awoke to the sunshine pouring through my window. The air in my room was cool and fresh, and it made my entire bedroom feel brand new.

Surprisingly, there wasn't too much on the news about the beetles. There was a mention about scientists gathering nearby to study a new species of insect that had been found, but that was about it.

"I wonder if that funny-talking foreign guy was making everything up," Lindsay said to me later that day. We were walking to the ice cream shop a few blocks away, and our plan was to hang out at a nearby park where a lot of our friends gathered.

I shook my head. "I don't think so," I said. "Did you see how serious that man and woman were? The ones in the trailer? And those dudes with the suits like Mr. Ivandrovich, the ones that used the spray to kill the escaping beetles? They were pretty serious about that."

"I guess you're right," Lindsay said. "It's crazy how all of that happened, right here, without very many people knowing about it. If what Mr. Ivandrovich was saying was true about the bacteria the beetles were carrying, everyone in the city would have panicked."

"Maybe that's why they wanted to stop the beetles before anyone found out about them," I said. "Maybe the panic would have been worse than the invading beetles."

The day was hot, and by the time we'd made it to the ice cream shop, a thin film of sweat was glazing my forehead.

"Ice cream is going to taste great," Lindsay said.

"Yeah," I agreed.

And we weren't the only ones with that idea. There was a line of about ten people, and we settled into our place behind a girl about my age with straight, jet-black hair. I looked up at the menu on the marquee.

"I'm going to have a waffle cone with chocolate ice cream and candy sprinkles," I said.

"That's what I'm going to have," the girl in front of me said, turning and smiling. I didn't recognize her, and I wondered if she lived in the area.

"Where are you from?" I asked.

The girl raised her eyebrows and smiled. "A long ways away," she said.

"Like, a few miles?" Lindsay asked.

The girl laughed. "A little more than that," she said. "I'm from Fairbanks, Alaska. I'm visiting my grandparents."

"Alaska?!?!" Lindsay and I gasped. I had never before met someone from that state. I know a little bit about it, but not much. I know that it's a huge mass of land and most of it is forest and that it gets pretty cold. And I know that much of Alaska is very wild, with grizzly bears and wolves and moose. But other than that, I didn't know too much about the state.

The girl nodded. "I'm Sasha Daniels," she said.

"I'm Hunter, and this is Lindsay," I said.

Just then, a bug flew up, hit Sasha in the nose, and flew off. Sasha didn't even flinch. It didn't seem to bother her at all.

"If that was a bee, he would have stung you," I said.

Sasha just smiled and shook her head. "I'm not afraid of bugs," she replied.

Lindsay and I looked at each other.

"Well, you might be," I said, "if you knew about the beetles that—"

"—I'm not afraid of beetles, either," Sasha interjected. "Not after what just happened to me."

Again, Lindsay and I looked at each other.

"What happened to you?" Lindsay asked.

"Well," Sasha said, "do you know what an anaconda is?"

I nodded. "It's some sort of really big snake," I said. "Don't they live in warm places like South America, or something?"

Sasha bobbed her head. "Most of them do," she said. "But there is a species of anaconda that lives in the snow and ice."

"What?" Lindsay said in disbelief. "That's not possible. Snakes are cold-blooded. They hibernate during the winter. I learned that at school."

Sasha shook her head. "Not these anacondas," she continued. "Let's get our ice cream, and I'll tell you what happened."

Sasha ordered her waffle cone with a double scoop of chocolate ice cream and candy sprinkles. I had the same, and Lindsay had a cherry snow cone. Carrying our cool treats, we walked to a picnic table in the shade and sat. Sasha began talking, and I couldn't believe what she was telling us. Lindsay and I listened, eyes wide, and nearly an hour went by as she told us all about her horrifying story of the arctic anacondas of Alaska . . . .

Next:

AMERICAN CHILLERS

AMERICA'S #1 SERIES FOR MAXIMUM CHILLS!

#42: Arctic Anacondas of Alaska

Continue on for a FREE preview!

Next!

1

My mom laughed.

"Really, Sasha," she said with a wary grin and a twinkle in her eye, "you don't believe any of those old trapper legends, do you?"

"Maybe," I replied with a shrug.

"Those stories about giant snakes were going around back when I was a little girl."

"First off, I'm not little," I huffed. "I'll be eleven in January, and that's only a month away. And second, my teacher says some of the old trapper stories about giant snakes might be true."

That's how the whole topic came up in the first place. Someone in Fairbanks—the city where we live—had once again reported seeing an enormous snake, living in the snow. There was a story about it in the newspaper and on television, and that's why some of my friends started talking about it at school.

Mom shook her head. "Those are just old wives' tales," she said.

"Well, they might be true," I said. "There's some guy in California, a snake specialist, and he says that it's possible that a species of snake evolved over millions of years, adapting to the cold and the snow and the ice. He says Alaska is the perfect place, because snakes like that could go undetected for years and years, and no one would find them."

Mom rolled her eyes and looked at the blanket of fresh snow beyond our living room window. It was still coming down, and the wind was blowing it around the window and through the trees.

"Well, you can believe what you want," Mom said, still smiling. "I guess I believed those stories when I was your age. Then I outgrew them when I realized that it's not possible for snakes of any size to live in the snow and ice."

Mom picked up her empty coffee mug and the book she was reading. She stood. "I have a few things to get done around here. What are you going to do today?"

"Trey is coming over. We're going to go snowshoeing."

"That sounds like fun. Looks like it's going to be another cold one today."

And Mom wasn't kidding. Fairbanks, Alaska, is known as 'America's Coldest City,' and there's a good reason for that. We get a ton of snow from October through April, and it can get really, really cold.

But Fairbanks isn't known for snakes, and certainly not giant snakes—anacondas—that can live in the snow and ice.

That is, until now.

2

Trey came over just after nine that morning. He lives about a mile away, and we both live on the same road. We don't live anywhere near the city limits, and there are no other houses around. We have no neighbors, other than the creatures of the forest. I know some people might find that kind of strange, but that's all I've known my entire life. I think most kids my age grow up and have a lot of friends to hang out with all the time, but not me. I have Trey, of course, but that's about it.

And that's fine with me. We live in the woods, and I love it. I hunt with my dad, I fish, and I play outdoors all the time, no matter what the weather. I build forts in trees. You might think that's weird for a girl, but I love it. And there are a lot of girls I know in Fairbanks that are just like me.

We live so far from the city that we don't have cable television, and the only telephone we have is an old wall unit in our living room. Other phones don't work where we live. I think that would drive most people crazy, but not my family. We spend most of our time outdoors. Dad works for a lumber mill, and Mom is a freelance writer for magazines. She mostly works at home where she can look after my little brother, Rocco, who's only two.

And Trey? He's been my best friend since I was little. We're the same age and in the same grade at school. He likes all the things I do, so we are always together and have a lot of cool adventures, and we spend most of our time in the woods.

Like today.

From my bedroom window, I saw Trey coming down our driveway, all bundled up with a rabbit fur hat, gloves, and a black snowsuit. He was plodding along on his snowshoes, and he was walking as normal and natural as can be. It was like he was born with snowshoes on his feet.

But what's really cool is that he made the snowshoes himself from willow branches, nylon rope, and old canvas. Even Trey will admit that they don't look very fancy, but they work great; better than what you can buy in store. Last year, he made a pair for my birthday. By far, I think that pair of snowshoes was the best gift I've ever received.

Trey looked up and saw me in my bedroom window. I waved, and he waved back. In ten minutes, we were both on our snowshoes, walking on the deep, newly-fallen snow. This year, it began snowing on October fifteenth. It was now almost Christmas, and there was more than two feet of snow on the ground, including a few inches of snow that fell last night . . . and it was still coming down.

"Did you see on the news about that guy who said he saw a giant snake not far from here?" I asked. I was leading the way, and Trey was following in my snowshoe tracks.

"Yeah," he said with a snicker. "What a nutcase. I think he—"

Trey stopped speaking, and I stopped walking and turned to look at him. He was staring at something in the snow a few feet away.

"What is it?" I asked.

Trey plodded to a spot a few feet away and knelt down. I joined him.

"Grizzly tracks," he said, pointing with his gloved hand. Then, he looked up. His serious eyes searched the forest, his gaze penetrated the trees and trunks. "Looks like he's running. Maybe chasing something. Pretty fresh tracks, too. Probably about an hour old."

We looked around warily. It was unusual to see bear tracks in the winter. Occasionally, grizzlies will come out of hibernation because they're hungry. But mostly, the only time you see them is during the spring, summer, or fall. And we don't see a lot of them in Fairbanks. Like most wild animals, grizzlies don't like people. They tend to stay away from us as much as possible.

But fresh tracks in the snow meant that somewhere, not far, was a grizzly bear. Oh, I wasn't worried . . . it was just something that we had to remember as we were hiking through the snow. It would be best if we saw him first, and stayed out of his way.

Again, we scoured the forest. The falling snow clumped on skeletal branches and dark green pine boughs, making everything look fresh and beautiful.

When I looked at Trey, he was smiling.

"What?" I asked.

"Giant snakes," he said with a laugh. "I'd be more concerned about grizzly bears than crazy stories about snakes that live in the snow."

But the day was just getting started. Very soon, Trey's opinion about giant snakes would change . . . when we both would realize that the old stories about snakes living in the ice and snow weren't just make-believe fairy tales. They were true.

The snakes were real.

And they were deadly.

3

We continued snowshoeing. On this day, we didn't really have any particular destination. Often, it's fun to simply head out into the woods to explore. Some days, you never know what you might find.

Like today.

We hiked until we came across a rapidly-flowing, narrow creek. We were familiar with the place, because we'd been in the forest so many times. I think we were in the woods more than we were at home, and we'd hiked to this particular creek dozens of times. The water rushed past, babbling and gurgling, moving too fast for the water to freeze.

"Look at all the tracks in the snow," Trey said, kneeling down near the water. "The animals have been busy this morning."

There were all sorts of tracks near the creek: deer, rabbit, squirrel, and a few that were unidentifiable because the newly-fallen snow had covered them up.

"Let's head upstream," Trey said as he stood. He pointed with his gloved hand. "We can cross the creek at the dead tree and go over to the pond."

Years ago, a large pine tree had fallen across the creek, and it was big enough to walk on. In the summer, we used it to cross the creek and hike to a large pond that was filled with huge northern pike and bass. Some of the fish we caught were so big that we had a hard time carrying them home.

Trey led the way. Although the snow was deep, our snowshoes made walking easy. And it was even more fun using the snowshoes Trey had made. I've seen snowshoes in some stores that cost more than one hundred dollars, but the ones Trey made were just as good. Maybe even better.

"Hey, wait up a second," I said.

Ahead of me, Trey stopped.

"What is it?" he asked.

"Look at this," I said, pointing at a hole in the snow.

Trey took a few steps toward me and looked at where I was pointing.

A couple of feet away was a round gap in the snow. It looked like a small cave or tunnel, big enough for a fat rabbit or maybe a big raccoon.

"Big deal," Trey said. "It's a hole in the snow. Probably from some animal."

"I know," I said, "but there's something strange about it."

"What?" Trey asked.

"I don't know," I replied. "But look." I took my glove off and pointed with a bare finger. "It looks like the snow is pushed up and out. Whatever made the hole came up from under the snow and went back down, because there aren't any tracks around."

"Like I said," Trey responded, "it's just some animal. A rabbit, most likely."

"Yeah, I guess you're right," I said.

But I still didn't believe that. Something wasn't right about the hole in the snow . . . and I didn't know what it was. I'd seen lots of holes that

201

were very similar, since there were many animals that burrowed into the snow.

But this is different, I kept thinking, as Trey and I began walking on our snowshoes again. There's something really strange about that hole.

Soon, I'd find out that I was right. I should have listened to that distant voice in my head, telling me that something was wrong.

Very wrong.

But by the time I would realize all of this, it would be far too late.

We hiked to where we planned to cross the fallen tree over the creek.

Or, we should have been able to cross. The tree trunk had been dislodged, pushed by swollen waters, and now it lay diagonal in the creek. Water swirled around and over it, and we knew right away that it would be too dangerous to try to cross. In the summer it wouldn't be so bad, because the worse thing that could happen was we might fall in and get wet.

But in the frigid winter? The last thing we wanted to do was fall into the raging creek. It was a long trek home, and hypothermia would set in before we'd be able to make it home. Without a doubt, we would freeze to death. Or one of us would, whoever was careless enough to risk trying to cross on the tree trunk.

"Looks like a dead end," I said. "At least until summer."

"Hey, no big deal," Trey said. "We don't even have to go to the pond. Let's just hike farther up the creek and see where it goes. We've been this far, but we've never followed the creek upstream from this point."

"Sounds good," I said, gazing at the forest around us. "I'm just glad we haven't seen any more grizzly bear tracks. But let's stay close to creek and not wander too far."

"Are you afraid of getting lost?" Trey asked with a smirk.

I shook my head, and my frosted bangs hit my cheeks. "No," I replied. "But it's snowing harder, and the fresh powder will cover our tracks. It's just common sense to follow the stream."

"Yeah, yeah," Trey said casually. He never worried about getting lost. Neither did I, really. But that was because I always took the right steps to make sure I wouldn't put myself in a position where I didn't know how to make it home.

Still, both of us were very comfortable in the woods. For us, the forest was just another home. We both hunted and fished, we both knew how to get around and survive on our knowledge and wits if we had to.

It was a good thing, too. Because very soon, we'd be putting all of our skills to the test—a test that was going to be a matter of life and death . . . and it all began with the finding of more strange tracks in the snow, and the discovery of a mysterious cave we'd never seen before.

ABOUT THE AUTHOR

Johnathan Rand has authored more than 90 books since the year 2000, with well over 5 million copies in print. His series include the incredibly popular **AMERICAN CHILLERS, MICHIGAN CHILLERS, FREDDIE FERNORTNER, FEARLESS FIRST GRADER,** and **THE ADVENTURE CLUB.** He's also co-authored a novel for teens (with Christopher Knight) entitled PANDEMIA. When not traveling, Rand lives in northern Michigan with his wife and three dogs. He is also the only author in the world to have a store that sells only his works: CHILLERMANIA is located in Indian River, Michigan and is open year round. Johnathan Rand is not always at the store, but he has been known to drop by frequently. Find out more at:

www.americanchillers.com